Also by Ann Carroll

Rosie's War

Ro[illegible]

Published by Poolbeg

Rosie's Century

Rosie's Century

ANN CARROLL

POOLBEG

Published by
Poolbeg Press Ltd
123 Grange Hill
Dublin 13, Ireland
E-mail: poolbeg@poolbeg.com
www.poolbeg.com

3 5 7 9 10 8 6 4 2

A catalogue record for this book is available from the British Library.

ISBN 1 85371 972 2

Cover design by Vivid Design
Set by Pat Hope
Printed by Cox & Wyman Ltd, Reading

About the Author

Ann Carroll is married with two children and lives in Dublin where she teaches English in Killinarden Community School. This is her fourth *Rosie* book published by Poolbeg. She has also written *Amazing Grace* (Poolbeg 1999).

For my husband Noel

Chapter 1

THE LETTER, dated Wednesday 27th March 1900, arrived at its destination a century later.

Rosie McGrath had just reached the bottom of the stairs when the thick envelope dropped onto the hall carpet. She was still in her pyjamas, because as soon as she got a bowl of rice crispies she was going back to bed.

"These are the most boring Easter holidays ever!" she thought. It was raining outside and had been for days. There was nothing to do. When she'd said as much to Mum, she'd got no sympathy.

"There's plenty for you to do," her mother had insisted.

"Like what?"

"Like spring-cleaning. Like hoovering the carpets, washing the floors, polishing the furniture."

Rosie had felt a bit weak. Mum was best avoided. Usually she was out at work, but had decided on a day off, "to sort out the house". This meant she would regard her daughter as a slave for the day. So hopefully Rosie could get her breakfast back to bed without being seen. There at least she could relax and read and not be tormented by housework.

The thought of it was exhausting.

Yawning, she picked up the letter, then blinked:

Miss Rosie McGrath
1, Innish Road,
Whitehall,
Dublin.

Her mouth stopped mid-yawn. The printed envelope looked very official. Who on earth was it from? It was far too thick to be a school report – unless she was in terrible trouble.

She tore it open. The letter-heading across the top of the first page caught her attention:

Macauley & Smith, Solicitors.

"Oh God!" Rosie wailed, wide awake now. "It's from lawyers. What have I done?"

Maybe Mr Brennan next door was suing her over the window in his greenhouse. But that had been an accident. She'd been mad at herself when she'd heard the tennis-ball crash through the glass. So mad she'd flung the racket over the wall as well. Of course she wasn't to know Mr Brennan was on the other side. Not until she heard him screech. And it wouldn't have been so bad if Mum had stayed in the house. Instead, after hearing the yelling, she'd rushed out at the very moment he'd flung the racket back.

For weeks afterwards Mum was complaining of a sore head. She'd blamed it all on her daughter and said Rosie could use her pocket money to pay for her aspirin and for the greenhouse and for Mr Brennan's stitches, though it turned out he was just bruised.

He'd been fairly friendly after that, though every time he saw her he pretended to duck which got a bit annoying. So why was he suing her now? And if it wasn't him, who was it?

Anyway, why should she be in trouble? Perhaps it was fantastic news. Maybe she'd won something. Maybe someone had left her a lot of money – though she couldn't think who.

Her mind in a whirl, Rosie decided breakfast could wait. Anyway, she could hear Mum wailing her favourite song in the kitchen:

While the bravest by far, in the ranks of the Tzar, was
Ivan Skavinzky Skavar,
Who caused such great woe when he trod on the toe of
Abdullah Bul Bul Amer.

Unable to think with the racket, Rosie made for her bedroom. Now she could read the letter in privacy. This way, if there was anything terrible in it, well, her parents didn't have to know, did they? At least not till she had time to plan how to tell them.

But in a million years she would never have guessed at the contents. Back under her duvet, head propped on the pillows, Rosie unfolded the pages once again. There must have been a dozen. Only the first sheet was from the solicitors. Anxiously she read:

Macauley & Smith, Solicitors. Established 1899.
Lower Leeson Street, Dublin 2

24. 3. 00

Dear Ms McGrath,

The enclosed letter has been on our files since 1900. In that year it was entrusted to the founders of this firm, Mister John Macauley and Mister Leo Smith, with instructions that it should be dispatched to your good self in March 2000.

It is our opinion that you were not alive one hundred years ago. Otherwise there would be no point to this excercise. Also, the records tell us your address did not exist then. Yet you and your house are there today. How the client knew this is beyond our understanding and is truly amazing.

We know from our files that Messrs Macauley and Smith tried to persuade the client against writing to a person who wasn't there, at a house that wasn't built. But he insisted his wishes must be carried out, providing our firm were still in business.

I am happy to say that our practice has grown from strength to strength over the century. And it has ever been our aim to satisfy our clients' wishes, even when those wishes might appear to be somewhat insane.

In dispatching the enclosed, we hope we have honoured all agreements in the matter.

Yours Sincerely,

Lorcan Macauley and Henry Smith.

Rosie read the letter three times before she understood the gist of it. Even then she wondered had she got it right.

"Are they telling me," she mused, "that someone wrote to me a hundred years ago?

And whoever it was didn't want me to get the letter till now?"

But who'd sent it? Her time-travels had brought her back to 1956, 1920 and 1870. She had never visited 1900. Who would know about her in that year and why had they written?

All she had to do was turn to the last page and the signature, but she hesitated.

Whoever had written it was long dead. It was as if a ghost were trying to communicate with her. Rosie shivered. Nobody would want a letter delivered after a hundred years unless they had something really important to say, would they?

Rosie closed her eyes. "It could be something dreadful," she thought.

She took a deep breath, then turned to the last page and looked. Her eyes widened and she almost laughed with delight.

"Joseph!" she breathed. "Joseph O'Neill!"

The relief was wonderful.

Her memories of the fourteen-year-old boy she'd met on her visit to 1870 came flooding back. How brave and clever he'd been, though he couldn't read or write. Joseph was her great-great-uncle and she'd gone back to help him. His parents were dead and he and his sister, Jane, were servants in Oak Park. When Rosie thought about her time there, she still felt rage at the way Cyril deCourcy had tried to destroy Joseph.

Then she giggled, remembering her great-great-uncle's reactions when he came back with her, briefly, to her own time. He'd been fascinated by the telly, chatting away to the person on *The Garden Show*. Then he'd put an egg in the microwave and got a terrible shock when it had exploded. There was nearly a disaster when Mr Brennan took him for a thief and grabbed him by the jacket. Luckily he'd slipped out of it and escaped.

Rosie still had that jacket. Though it was old and shabby, she'd kept it as a memento.

He had been great fun, she thought.

She had often wondered how life had turned out for him. Now she had a chance to find out.

In 1900 Joseph was forty-four years old. Such a lot must have happened to him.

She turned to the letter.

Chapter 2

St John's,
Sandymount Avenue
Tuesday 27th March 1900

Dear Rosie.

It's strange to be writing a letter that won't arrive for a hundred years, if it arrives at all. Tomorrow I shall leave this into my solicitors with instructions to send it in 2000. I'm pretty certain you'll be in Whitehall then.

You changed my life in 1870 and I thought you'd like to know what's happened to me since. One way of telling you would be to visit you, but my gift for time-travel has disappeared. Perhaps it's because I'm an adult or perhaps it's because my last journey to your time used up all my power. Anyway, I know it's gone.

The other day I took the tram to Drumcondra and made my way up the hill to Whitehall. Most of it is fields with the odd farm cottage. With all the greenery around me, I had to guess where your house will be. Then, standing in the middle of a big meadow, I concentrated and called your name.

For a moment I thought it was going to work, as time seemed to change. There were different sounds, like the rumble of those lorries that scared me so much the last time. I opened my eyes and

I could see the outline of houses and a street. But they faded and so did the noise and I was alone. This letter is my only way to communicate and I hope it will reach you.

So, what's happened in my life?

Well, when you left, Mr Harvey, the butler, taught me and Jane and Cook to read and write. As we got better, he would write sentences about how wonderful Cook's meals were, or what a fine person she was. Or silly rhymes. I remember one in particular:

With oatmeal all the way from Norwich
Cook makes the most exciting porridge
And it certainly ain't in her
To create a nasty dinner.
As for her face, I tell no lie
'Tis beautiful as apple-pie!

Then I'd have to read the lines out, or Jane. We might have laughed, except Mr Harvey was deadly serious. We thought Cook might hit him for comparing her to an apple-pie (something he did quite often) but not at all. The poor woman couldn't stop smiling and her face would blaze like the fire. I'm sure other children's reading lessons weren't like ours.

She remembered you with fondness, Rosie. She said she was quite relieved to find out you weren't a Brannigan, since the Brannigans were brainless. You were the strangest person she'd ever met, she said, and used constantly to wonder who you were and where you'd come from. Of course I never told her. She'd never have believed me.

She and Mr Harvey married in 1871. They went to Boston and the last I heard they were rearing two fine children and had opened a fancy restaurant. Funny, I never thought of Cook as young enough to have children.

As for my sister, Jane, she got married from Oak Park and Lady de Courcy made her the gift of a small holding in County Meath where she and her husband and family live now, though I know she'd like to settle in Dublin one day.

For my part, I left Oak Park when I turned fifteen and joined Her Majesty's Indian army.

It was a good life and when my regiment transferred to Burma, I was promoted to captain. Not bad for a gardener's boy, hey?

I left the army and stayed on in Burma for another eight years, making a lot of money from a rubber plantation and marrying my old colonel's daughter, Louisa. When our twin boys were eleven, we decided to come back to Ireland. Now we live in Dublin, where I started an import-export business, with a second office in Cork. It gives us a tidy income.

So you see, Rosie, I have done well. And it's all thanks to you. If you hadn't come back that time, I'd have ended up in prison, regarded as a common criminal.

"I can't imagine Joseph with children," Rosie mused, "or as a business man."

She remembered the boy she'd known. He couldn't read or write and he was one of the lowest servants in Oak Park. But he was brave, kind and intelligent. "I'm glad he got what he deserved," she thought and turned back to his letter.

I've been thinking about you a lot recently, Rosie, not least because my boys are about the same age as you. They're a right pair. Always up to tricks and always in trouble. Henry and Edward they're called, though their mother says they should've been christened Disaster and Destruction, because of the scrapes they get into.

Last week they scared the wits out of Mollie, the kitchen maid. She believes in ghosts. William got under the kitchen table just before she sat down to tea. The table-cloth hid him from view. By moving a strong magnet underneath the table, he got the teapot to travel along the top. In the meantime Edward moaned from behind the door. The poor girl thought she was haunted. She was in tears and said she'd have to leave the house. Of course the boys were sorry at once. They were especially sorry when their mother told them they'd have to do all

Mollie's jobs if she went. They've never been keen on cleaning and scrubbing, polishing brass or peeling potatoes. The thought upset them mightily. I never heard two boys apologise so often or so humbly. In the end Molly stayed.

They're not bad fellows really and they never mean any harm. I think you'd like them, Rosie. They even look a bit like you. Brown eyes and fair hair runs in the family. You'll hardly get to meet them though. It's not likely they'll live to the year 2000. They'd be one hundred and twelve. A bit ancient, don't you think?

Rosie was struck by a sudden thought. "I wonder what relation William and Edward are to me? I mean, if Joseph is my great-great-uncle and they're his sons, are they my great uncles? But then aren't great-uncles the brothers of great-grandparents? And Henry and Edward are the nephews of Jane, my great-great-grandmother, so that means they're the cousins, *not* the brothers, of my great-grandmother. And if they were her first cousins, does that make them my third or maybe my fourth cousins? So. Are they uncles or cousins?"

Her head began to throb. She gave up trying to puzzle it out and turned to the letter, once again, her eyes widening as she read.

By the way, do you remember Tom Hannigan? He was the footman in Oak Park. He was quite hot on Irish freedom. You might recall a quarrel he had with Mr Harvey. He supported the Fenians and Mr Harvey did not.

Tom is in his sixties now. His health isn't good and he lives with his sister and her family in Monkstown. Well, an extraordinary thing has happened. Last week he visited me with the strangest story. And in a way, it involves you.

All those years ago, in Oak Park, an acquaintance of Tom's came to visit him. A man called Donnelly, who had Fenian connections. He said he was on the run from the police for terrorist activities. He asked Tom to mind a paper for him – a page on which was written a set of clues showing the whereabouts of a box of gold sovereigns. These coins had been given to the movement by a wealthy sympathiser. But times were dangerous, the Fenians had scattered and the money had been hidden. The clues were drawn up and given to Donnelly for safekeeping. The gold would be used to fight the cause another day.

At least that was what Donnelly told Tom.

But it turned out to be a false tale that had nothing to do with the cause. Donnelly had robbed and murdered for the clues and knew the police were catching up. He also knew Tom would do a lot for the Fenians, so he gave him that cock-and-bull story. He expected to be arrested and questioned, but with no trace of the paper he thought he'd never be charged. He was sure he'd be back in a few weeks. In the meantime Tom must keep the paper in a safe place. If the police knew of his link with Donnelly, they would question and search him.

Rosie, you'll never guess where Tom hid the clues. No one would guess. Who would ever think of looking in the seams of an old jacket belonging to a gardener's boy? My jacket, Rosie. One night, when I'd left it in the servants' cloakroom, Tom carefully unpicked the stitches, hid the paper in the lining and sewed up the seam again. That was the jacket I wore to your time and left there, the one your neighbour, Mr Brennan, pulled off me when he found me in your house and thought I was a robber.

Life takes peculiar turns and we never know what's in store for us.

The day after you left Oak Park forever, Tom was summoned to Sligo, where his father was seriously ill. By the time he returned a few months later, I'd gone to England and joined the army. At this stage he knew the truth about Donnelly, decided the sovereigns were tainted and it was better to forget all about the clues.

As for Donnelly, he was caught all right and charged with murder. He didn't know it, but someone had seen him commit the crime and came forward as a witness. He got thirty years imprisonment and was lucky not to have been hanged.

In January this year, he was released. What was the first thing he did? Went looking for Tom. It took him some weeks. He turned up on Tom's doorstep in Monkstown demanding his paper. Imagine! After thirty years, he expected Tom to still have it for him. Well, Tom told him what he'd done with it and said the jacket must've been thrown in the dustbin long ago. (And I daresay that's exactly what Mr *Brennan did with it.)*

Do you think Donnelly believed him? No. He thought Tom was trying to cheat on him. He said he hadn't endured all those years in prison to have nothing when he came out. He wanted what was his by right! And he was prepared to kill again if he had to. The man ranted on and on. He wouldn't listen. He even started threatening Tom's sister and her family. Then he said I must be in on it too and he would see us both in hell unless we returned his paper. He got more and more angry. In the end they had to get a policeman before he would leave their doorstep.

Tom had read about my return from Burma in The Irish Times. *So knowing where I lived, he called to tell me the sorry tale. Not that he thought I'd have the clues, but he wanted to warn me against Donnelly. Tom thinks prison has made the man even more dangerous and that he might be insane.*

Of course it wasn't long before Donnelly turned up here. I told him I hadn't got what he wanted and eventually he went away. He hasn't been here since.

I reckon the poor man has come to his senses and realises there's no hope of finding a paper that disappeared thirty years ago. He's probably decided to forget about it.

If he does call again, I shall tell him I left his clues in the future, at an address that doesn't yet exist, with a person who isn't yet alive. No doubt he'll think he could never match my madness and it's best to leave such a raving maniac alone.

Well, that's my news, Rosie. I only wish you could write a letter to the past and tell me about yourself, but time doesn't work like that. Still, it's good to let you know how you changed my life for the better.

I still remember that week in 1870 as though it were yesterday. Even after thirty years I think I would know you again. Your face is still vivid.

And I remember how afraid you were of being trapped in 1870. Time-travel has its dangers. I wish it were possible for us to meet. This letter is a poor substitute for seeing you.

All the Best and may your life be a happy one.

Your loving relative,
Joseph O'Neill.

P.S. The whole of Dublin is busy preparing for the Queen's visit next week. But I'm sure you know all about it from your history books.

Rosie took a long, deep breath. She had never heard of the Queen's visit and it didn't interest her. What did interest her was Joseph's jacket which was hanging in her wardrobe. Mr Brennan had not thrown it in the bin. He'd given the jacket to Mum who'd considered her daughter very strange indeed when she'd wanted to keep it.

"Why would anyone want a criminal's jacket?" she'd said. "Except maybe the police. And even *they* didn't want this one! It's grotty, Rosie. It looks ancient and it's probably full of fleas. It's baggy and saggy. Now, I know young people like funny clothes, but really! If you ever wore this disgusting object, I'd be forced to disown you. It should be dumped."

Swallowing hard, Rosie had managed to ignore all the insults. Inside she was raging. Joseph's jacket might be old and a bit raggy, but at least it wasn't like a set of traffic-lights, all shiny and lurex like the one her mother was so proud of and which she, Rosie, had luckily left in Oak Park.

Of course her mother would have a fit if she said any of that. Instead she told her, "That old jacket could come in handy if I get a part in the school play."

"Could it? Will you be playing a scarecrow?" Pleased with her little joke, Mom had cheered up and made no more objections.

Rosie gazed at the wardrobe. That seedy jacket held the clues to treasure hidden one hundred and thirty years ago. A box of golden sovereigns. How exciting it would be to find them. Donnelly had killed for this fortune. He'd been willing to do so again. "He'll see us both in hell" according to Joseph's letter. The words jolted Rosie. Donnelly sounded very dangerous.

What had happened back in 1900? Had Donnelly come after Joseph? Had he harmed him? Tried to murder him, even?

There was only one way to find out. She would have to go back to 1900.

Rummaging in a drawer, Rosie found a nail-scissors. Swiftly she took the jacket from its hanger and felt carefully along the seams. On the inside arm, just above the elbow, the material seemed thicker and she heard a slight rustle. Unpicking the threads she drew out a folded page. It crackled with age when she opened it out. The once black ink had faded to grey and the paper felt as if it might crumble. It was after all a hundred and thirty years old.

Almost afraid to breathe, Rosie read the clues. There were five, neatly numbered:

1. *Mac may not stay in the Monkstown sweet shop, but Jones must be added.*
2. *The foreign photographer with Lawrence is Bob who?*
3. *In Glasnevin Cemetery, beneath the divided elm, find the last word for Battling Henry.*
4. *At the king's harbour find the key beneath the first stand where the iron circles on the right.*
5. *Where furniture is made, beneath the pale boards.*

Rosie's first thought was that the clues were the work of a lunatic. Someone who liked making up mad sentences with no sense. But then clues were supposed to be mysterious, weren't they? Otherwise they wouldn't be clues, they'd just be a set of instructions. And Donnelly would hardly have acted as he did for five daft lines of writing!

"They must mean something," Rosie sighed. There was a word for clues like this. She racked her brains. "*Cryptic*. That's it. When no one has a flamin' clue what the clues mean! Great."

And in 1900 they were already thirty years out of date. Could the riddle be solved after that length of time? And would the hiding-place be unchanged? If the treasure was in the ground, it could be all ploughed up. Or someone might have found it. Or there might be houses and roads on top of it.

Rosie was getting a headache. There was no point thinking about problems that might not exist. Not when she had real problems to think about. Like how she was going to leave home for a week and not tell her parents where she was going. "I mean I can hardly say 'Mum, I won't be here for a week, I'm just popping back to 1900'."

For one thing, her mother did not believe in time-travel. So if Rosie mentioned it, she'd probably suggest a visit to the doctor and a nice long rest. For another thing, she always had to know Rosie's whereabouts. Even when she stayed overnight with her friend Helena Gavin, who lived on the other side of Dublin, Mum always rang her house to make sure it was all right. So how on earth was she going to fool her?

Rosie had made three visits to the past and was really lucky not to have been found out.

She could never in a million years have convinced her parents about where she'd gone. They'd definitely have thought she was raving. A couple of times she'd nearly been caught out. The school-trip was a useful excuse last time, but school was closed now for the Easter holidays.

What cover could she use this time? It would have to be foolproof.

Chapter 3

LOST IN thought, she did not hear the phone ring downstairs. Her mother took the call and shouted, "Rosie. Rosie!" Dear God, the child was deaf! Or more likely had earplugs in, listening to her music.

"Rosie!" she roared. No reply.

"Ro-o-o-sie! Phone call. Helena!" she shrieked and this time her daughter heard. Placing the page carefully on the bed, she raced downstairs.

"There's no need to roar, Mum. I'm not deaf." But Mrs McGrath was already out of range, remembering a pot she'd left on the cooker.

"I was just thinking about you," Rosie told her friend.

"The holidays are so *boring*," Helena moaned.

"They are. And we only got them yesterday. Still, it's better than school. If we were in school, what would we be doing now?" She looked at her watch."Ten past eleven."

"We'd be on toilet-break." Helena sounded regretful. "We'd be chatting. We'd be slagging Maisie Mulligan for smoking in the toilets. She always goes mad when you tell her smoking stunts her growth."

Maisie Mulligan was one of the tallest girls in the school, even though she was only a first-year.

"You're forgetting," Rosie said. "It's Tuesday. So after toilet-break, we have PE And Mr Murray says if it's the last thing he does he's going to get us fit and we'd be going on our five-mile cross-country run, so we would. And we'd be dead. He should be arrested for torture."

For a moment they thought about Mr Murray, their tutor and PE teacher. Normally, he was deadly, great fun. But every so often he got a bee in his bonnet about the horrible state of class 1E's fitness. Then he'd ban sweets and crisps, or make them run up and down the school stairs fifty times. Cross-country running was his latest.

Helena sniffed, "Well, maybe we are better off on holidays then. Anyway, I didn't ring to talk about school. You know our holiday cottage?"

"The one in the middle of nowhere?"

Helena's parents called it their getaway home. A refuge from the busy lives they led in the city.

"It's in Wexford," Her friend said. "And it's not that bad. It's near the sea. We're going there tomorrow."

"The sea's not very nice at the end of March," Rosie said. "And you told me there isn't another house in sight and not a town for miles and you've no electricity and no telly and no phone."

"Oh. Did I?" Helena sounded depressed. "So you won't come with us?"

"I didn't know you were asking me." Suddenly Rosie's mind clicked into gear and ideas began to rev up.

"Isn't that why I'm ringing? Listen, Rosie, it's not that bad. At least it won't be if you come. There's plenty of places to explore and it's really cosy when Dad lights the open fire at night and the candlelight is magic and there's a range for cooking the food – oh please say you'll come, Rosie. Please!"

"And there's definitely no phone?"

"No. But we'll only be away for a week and –"

"What about a mobile phone? Will there be one of them?"

Her friend sighed, "Afraid not. I've got very strange parents and they don't wan't to be contacted at all. Look, if you're that desperate, I'll sneak their mobile with me."

"No, don't! It's great no one can reach you. Really cool and –"

"Deadly! You'll come. Put your mum on the phone then and let mine talk to her. Go on, Rosie, before you change your mind."

"Listen, Helena, there's something I want to tell you."

It was too late. Her friend had gone to get her mother. Rosie fetched hers.

Five minutes later it was all arranged. She was to be over at Helena's house by ten o'clock next morning.

"We won't be able to give you a lift across, " Mum said. "I've to be in work early and your dad has to meet some business clients first thing. We'll be away all day."

"I'm only bringing a rucksack," Rosie said. "I can get the bus. And I'll get it home as well."

Rosie spent the rest of the day avoiding housework and making plans. She hated letting Helena down. That evening, while her parents were watching telly in the breakfast room, she rang around her friends from school. Not one of them was keen to go to a remote cottage for a week. In fact most of them seemed to think it would be a form of torture.

In the end, David Byrne said he'd go, after she'd bribed him. "But only as a favour to you, Rosie. And because you're giving me an Oasis CD and your dad's old soccer ball with *Georgie Best* signed on it and a six-pack of coke as well as a huge Toblerone. I'd do this for no one else. And I'll be calling around to collect in an hour, so have it all ready. Otherwise it's no deal."

David could never resist making a deal. But he was good

fun. And Helena liked him, though she might be a bit startled to find he was going to stay with her. And as for Helena's mum! But Rosie would deal with that problem next morning.

She got Dad's old soccer ball out of the garage and brought down her Oasis cd. Then she sneaked a six-pack of coke into the hall.

The huge Toblerone was in the fridge. Her dad loved Toblerone and she knew he was looking forward to opening this one. Usually he'd leave the bar for hours, saying it tasted much nicer that way. He drove Rosie mad, as she always helped him eat it.

This time she hoped he'd forget about it till tomorrow. On the other hand, if he saw her carrying it away he might get hysterical. How to get it through the breakfast room?

She pushed the giant bar up the sleeve of her jumper and held it in place with her other hand. It was so big it gave her a funny-looking elbow. She went through the breakfast room with folded arms. But her parents hardly noticed her. They were glued to some news programme. "Funny,"she thought, "when I watch telly like that they say I'm turning into a zombie."

Rosie could see David Byrne's outline through the glass in the front door. She opened it before he could knock. Putting her finger to her lips, she piled the booty into his arms and, leaving the door ajar, walked down the drive with him.

"My parents don't know I'm giving you this. I don't want them to see. Especially my dad. He's very fond of Toblerone."

"Fair enough. I bet he'd kill you if he knew you were giving away his Georgie Best soccer ball."

Rosie said nothing. At one of the neighbours' walls, David stopped and set down his goods. "I can't wait to have a proper look at the ball. It's a bit shabby." He held it up, studying the signature.

"It's old," Rosie muttered.

"Mmm. My dad has Georgie Best's book. He bought a signed copy. The signature doesn't look like this."

"A ball is harder to write on than a book," Rosie said. "That's probably why the signature is funny."

He wasn't convinced. "Maybe. And is that why he got the spelling all wrong too? Is that why he put 'Gorgy Beast' instead of "Georgie Best'?"

Rosie seized the ball. He was right. She'd been in too much of a hurry.

"And why does the writing look new when the ball is so old? You said Georgie Best signed this. You were lying."

"I was not!" Rosie was indignant. "I said it had Georgie Best signed on it. I never said who wrote it. If you're changing your mind, you can give it back – and everything else."

He was accusing. "You also said you'd give me a six-pack of coke."

"That is a six-pack of coke. What do you think it is? Vinegar?"

"What do I think it is? I think it's Diet Coke. I *know* it's Diet Coke. I don't *like* Diet Coke!"

Rosie was grim, "Well, my mother does, and these are hers. You can hump off, David Byrne. Complaining about everything. You're one sad character! Gimme back my dad's Toblerone and my Oasis."

Swiftly he gathered up the goodies. "I will not. A deal is a deal. You tell Helena I'll see her in the morning."

He practically ran down the road.

Rosie packed for her journey. From past experience she knew that if the time switch was successful, what she was wearing would change. She'd find herself in clothes that fitted in with the year and with the people she was visiting. There was no point packing anything modern. She'd never get to wear jeans or sweatshirts or trainers. She remembered the awful uniform she'd had to wear in1956, and the confirmation suit that weighed a ton.

1920 had been worse, stuck in a raggedy dress, a man's jacket and horrible knickers.

And that maid's hat and apron she'd had on in 1870 had made her look like an imbecile. She sighed. The clothes might be different this time but she was sure they'd still be disgusting.

What would she bring? Mum would ask awkward questions if her rucksack looked empty. She put a lot of knickers at the bottom. That gave it some weight. Over them she threw in some biros, markers, a notebook. Raiding the kitchen presses, she took Kit-Kat, Mars bars, crisps, pot noodles, and two cans of proper coke. These filled the rest of the space. In one of the side pockets she placed a torch, Joseph's letter and the clues. In the other she put some discs and her CD player. Almost as small as a disc-man, it had one advantage. Earphones were optional, so lots of people could listen at the same time. Dad had used it last and there was one of his CDs in it. Too lazy to put it back in his collection, she left it and zipped up the rucksack.

That was it. Now she was ready for her adventure. As ready as she'd ever be.

To go back one hundred years was a huge journey. It was like travelling to a distant land. The people would be like foreigners, their way of life completely different. Everytime she'd returned to the past, Rosie felt she'd arrived not just from another country, but from another planet. At least this time she'd know Joseph. It should make things easier. And it would be great to see him again.

Next morning Dad never mentioned his Toblerone, so he hadn't missed it yet. He and Mum rushed around the house, getting everything together for their meeting. They gave Rosie pocket money for the week, hoped she'd have a good time and then they were gone.

Rosie rang Helena. She'd rehearsed her excuse, but hoped her friend wouldn't ask too many questions. However, it was Helena's mum who answered and Rosie's voice went hoarse with panic.

"Oh God, it's Mrs Gavin! I just rang to say I won't be able to go away with you."

It was one thing to mislead her friend. Her friend's mother might be far more difficult.

"Is that you, Rosie? You sound odd. Oh dear, Helena will be disappointed."

"It's my uncle Joseph. It's ages since I've seen him. Then he contacted me yesterday. So I'm going to stay with him for the week instead of with you. Is that all right?"

"Well, of course you must stay with your uncle. Where does he live?"

"Sandymount. He's back from Burma, you see. With his two sons. William and Edward. They're boys. Well, they would be with those names." Rosie knew she was gabbling, but couldn't stop herself. "I suppose they're my cousins, though I'm not sure. They could be some kind of uncles. It's a bit complicated." She trailed off.

"Mmmmm," said Mrs Gavin. The child didn't sound at all well. Her voice was strange and she wasn't making much sense. "Listen Rosie, maybe you're coming down with the flu. Are you feeling feverish?"

"No. Though I had a headache yesterday. I was thinking."

"Yes? What were you thinking?"

"Lots of things. That's how I got the headache."

"My goodness. Well, you must be careful then. You don't want to strain your head. So look after yourself and enjoy your week. And don't worry about whether your cousins are your uncles. I'm sure they're perfectly normal."

"I don't think so. My uncle says they're disaster and destruction."

"Mmmmm," Mrs Gavin murmured again."What age are they?"

"Around twelve."

"Ah. Twelve-year-old boys. That explains your uncle's description.They sound perfectly normal and charming. Helena will be very sorry you can't come with us, Rosie."

"That's what I thought, so I rang David Byrne and he said he'll go. He'd really like to, if that's all right."

"Wonderful. I know David well and Helena likes him. His mother is in my Bridge club. I'll just phone her now."

Suddenly Rosie knew how to get her own back on David for so being ungrateful.

"There's one thing you ought to know about him, Mrs Gavin"

"What's that?"

"He loves everything outdoors. Like climbing and walking. He goes swimming in the forty-foot every weekend. But he'll be too shy to tell you himself. He'll just think he's putting you out. So I thought I'd mention it."

"Well, you are very kind, Rosie. I'll make sure he gets to do lots of activities. The sea is only yards away. And we've plenty of spare swimsuits if he forgets his own. He can swim every day. I must say he's very hardy. The water is freezing at this time of the year."

"He loves the sea all year round, Mrs Gavin."

Rosie grinned. If there was one thing David hated, it was physical excercise. He was mad about soccer all right, but only on the telly. She'd like to see his face when Helena's mum gave him the spare pair of togs or he was forced to go on a five-mile walk. Was she being really mean? Rosie remembered the way he'd complained about the coke and the football. He deserved a bit of a shock.

"Now, Rosie, take a couple of aspirin and you'll feel much better." Mrs Gavin was saying. "I'll tell Helena what's happened. She'll understand."

"Thanks, Mrs Gavin." Where on earth had Helena's mum got the idea she wasn't well? Rosie put the phone down.

She checked her watch. It was nine thirty. Leaving her rucksack in the hall, she had a last look round. Each time she'd gone back Rosie had been scared that she'd be trapped in the past. It had comforted her to remember home. Always she'd had a sense of belonging only to her own time. If she stayed in the past she'd lose her family and friends. On her last trip she'd been afraid for a brief time that it might be impossible to get home, and the sense of dread had been awful. She'd felt as though she'd lost her future, that her life had been thrown off its proper path and it no longer had any direction. It was unbearable. But then her gift had worked and she'd come home.

Would she be as lucky this time? She memorised details of the house and garden so that they would be strong in her mind and she could focus clearly on them when she wanted to return.

Rosie got the Number 3 bus from Whitehall to Sandymount Village. She had to ask the way from there. The weather had changed and the day was bright and warm. She walked by the railings of the village green, past the shops and the cafe, then turned right, up by the redbrick Victorian houses.

She was looking for a name plate to tell her she had arrived at St John's and she found it beyond the railway crossing. It was a corner house, with large basement windows and granite steps leading up to the red door. Late Spring flowers filled the garden. The sun gleamed on the gravel path and there were climbers growing up the side wall. The red brick looked warm and welcoming.

It was eleven o'clock. The road was busy enough with cars. An elderly couple were out walking their dog, on their way to the village, and a jogger kept a steady pace towards Ballsbridge. A man on a mobile phone was getting into his parked car.

A woman came down the steps of St John's. She glanced at the young girl in the fleece jacket and jeans, fair hair tied back, rucksack over her shoulder. "Are you looking for someone? Can I help you?"

"No, thanks," Rosie said.

The woman smiled and went to her car. Rosie watched as she rummaged at the dashboard.

The street grew quiet. The hustle and bustle had eased for a few minutes. Apart from herself and the woman in the car, there was no one in sight now.

Rosie fixed the date on her watch to 28.3.1900. She took Joseph's letter from the side pocket of the rucksack.

Holding it firmly in her hand, she closed her eyes. "Joseph," she murmured, "where are you?"

The place was silent now, but she sensed no change, no shift in time. She opened her eyes to the same streetscape. The woman in the nearby car was now looking through some papers, frowning with concentration.

If she were to make the journey back, Rosie needed something extra. She looked at Joseph's letter. It seemed to her that some of the words were no longer faded and the blue ink was fresh on the page.

Two phrases stood out: *I've been thinking about you a lot recently and I wish it were possible for us to meet.*

Closing her eyes, Rosie tried again, murmuring the sentences over and over as if she were the one who had written them.

She heard someone on the steps. There was a pause and the rattle of keys and time shook slightly. The air grew a little warmer and the street was absolutely still. Whoever it was – a man – began singing as he fumbled with the keys. The words seemed to come from a great distance.

"Daisy, Daisy give me your answer do. I'm half crazy all for the love of you."

Then the voice stopped. Rosie blinked and looked up.

There was no one on the steps. Swinging around, she almost wept to see that nothing had altered. It was not going to happen. Yet she could have sworn there'd been a change. And although the song was familiar, it wasn't modern, it was old.

She had to try again. This time she must use all her strength. The letter wasn't enough to make contact with Joseph. She needed something else. Swiftly she pulled his jacket from her rucksack and draped it around her shoulders. Taking a deep breath she focused:

I wish it were possible for us to meet, Joseph. I've been thinking a lot about you recently.

Again and again she said this.

She heard the sound of a heavy key in the lock.

The door swung open and then there was silence as the man stopped what he was doing.

He heard his name and frowned. "Who's there?" he called.

He could see no one, yet the voice was becoming more distinct. *"Joseph. I've been thinking a lot about you recently. I wish it were possible for us to meet."*

The words were familiar. Not only the words but the voice. Intently he listened, then caught his breath and took the steps two at a time onto the pavement.

"Rosie! Is it you, Rosie? You've come back." He looked around him wildly, trying to fix the exact source of the voice.

Then it was absolutely clear and present, and sounding a little shy. He turned around.

The woman in the car at last had found what she was looking for. She smiled in triumph and glanced up. That kid was still there. What was she doing? She hadn't been wearing that mouldy old jacket a few minutes ago. And now she looked as if she were going to faint, eyes closed, swaying. Better to catch her before she fell.

She pushed open the car door and was getting out whe there was a sudden rush of air. Straightening up, she could not believe her eyes.

The girl was gone.

She looked up and down the street in bewilderment.

No sign of her.

She had disappeared into thin air.

Chapter 4

ROSIE BARELY had time to take in the tall fair-haired man with the smiling eyes before she was distracted. Joseph stretched a hand towards hers and she loosened her grip on the letter. A sudden gust of wind lifted the pages high into the air while the envelope dropped between the grids of a shore in the gutter. It mixed with the liquid mud beneath and slowly disappeared. Above the roofs of Sandymount Avenue the pages hovered a moment, fluttered, then floated out of sight. She ran across the road, scanning the skyline. It was no good. They were gone.

Joseph had followed, anxious not to lose her.

"It's your letter," Rosie told him. "It flew out of my hand."

"My letter?"

"Yes."

Joseph looked so astounded Rosie felt obliged to explain. "The one dated 1900. You told me how you got on after Oak Park, and all about Donnelly."

"I know exactly what letter you mean, Rosie, because I've just left it into my solicitors for delivery in one hundred years' time. So if they have it, how could you have it? It can't be in two places at once."

"But that's the point. I don't have it. It disappeared on me, so it must be where you left it."

"But that means you've received a letter that hasn't been sent yet."

They were silent, both trying to grasp the mysteries of time.

In the end Joseph concluded, "Perhaps it's better not to question what happens. We'll never understand it anyway. It seems more grateful somehow to accept time-travel as a gift, instead of trying to find an explanation."

Rosie nodded, then smiled, "We haven't even said 'hello' properly."

They looked at each other, taking stock.

Joseph was a good deal taller and a good deal older than when they'd last met. He was also better dressed, wearing an excellent dark suit with a gold watch-chain across his waistcoat. The dark bowler hat and the silver-topped walking stick added to the impression of a well-off gentleman. His face was tanned and his dark eyes crinkled.

He sighed, "It's amazing, Rosie. You look exactly the same. Well, except for the clothes. They're much nicer. Apart from that funny-looking jacket."

She became aware of what she was wearing. A dark green dress not quite ankle-length, with soft collar and long sleeves; dark green knee socks and sturdy laced-up boots. That much was okay. That much she could put up with. But what had she on over the dress? "Flamin' heck!" It was a kind of fancy white sleeveless overall with a lot of puckered stitching on the chest and frills instead of a proper hem. There was enough material in it for a parachute. And topping it all was Joseph's old jacket, which he obviously didn't recognise.

"What is this over-thing, Joseph?"

"It's a smock. To keep your dress clean." He grinned. "Your hat is lovely too."

"Hat?" She put a hand up. She had on a huge beret. "Oh my God. I'm wearing a pancake!"

He laughed. "You haven't changed."

But *he* had. He was a stranger, an adult, his voice deeper, his appearance well-off.

"I can't believe it, Joseph. It's only a few months since I've seen you and you've got so –" She stopped.

"So old," he finished. "It's a few months for you, but thirty years for me. Time is odd." He smiled. "You'll get used to me."

Would she? She could not understand her disappointment. After all, she'd known he would be older. She should have realised he would not be recognisable.

"I can't believe this street either," she said, suddenly noticing the extreme changes and glad of the distraction. "It's so quiet. No traffic."

A carriage waited at one of the houses, the horses standing patiently, one feeding from his nosebag, the other drinking from the stone water-trough at the edge of the pavement. Her ears tuned in to the sound of clopping hooves from the next street and she heard the clang of a distant tram as it shunted to a halt.

"Oh, we have one or two motor cars," Joseph told her. "Very unsafe they are. And so fast. At least ten miles an hour."

"Really?" She was sarcastic. "It's a wonder the drivers aren't arrested for dangerous driving. "

"Oh, they are," Joseph said. "Often."

"For heaven's sake! A bicycle could go faster than that!"

"But a bicycle won't frighten the horses!" Joseph told her.

At that moment two bikes came shuddering around the corner, solid tyres bouncing the owners, who sweated as they pedalled the ton weights. Rosie felt hot looking at them. "I don't think they'd do well in the *Tour de France*,'" she murmured.

"Let's go inside," Joseph said. "You must meet the family. Louisa will be in the morning room and I'll get Henry and Edward down from the nursery."

Before she could answer he had bounded up the steps. In no time he'd opened the door and stepped into the hall. Rosie had no choice but to follow.

The hall was long and wide, a large oak table on one side with a stuffed falcon, wings spread, under a huge glass dome. There was a stand alongside, with pots of plants and further down was a grandfather clock. In an alcove, near some steps leading downwards, stood a brass gong. The wallpaper was dark red. Two oriental rugs rested on the highly polished wooden floor. All the furnishing was solid, meant to last for centuries.

Joseph was calling the family: "Louisa! Henry! Edward! Come into the hall."

"What are you going to tell them?"

He had no time to reply as two boys galloped towards them.

"Pa, you're late!"

"And you promised we could help with the bunting!"

"We wanted to do the lampposts. Me and William are good at climbing lampposts. We could do the whole avenue." Then they both stopped, noticing Rosie. They stared at her with open curiosity and Rosie stared back.

They were tall, both brown-eyed and fair-haired. But they were not identical twins. Small differences distinguished them. One had a slightly narrower face, a more serious expression and his hair flopped over one eye. The other boy's hair was shorter and seemed to stand on end a little as if he were always running a hand through it. His eyes were merry and he had no stillness, even now jigging around.

"Rosie, this is Henry – he's the one who looks more serious, but don't be deceived. And that's Edward." He leaned forward and ruffled Edward'd hair, leaving it even more spiky.

"And who is this young lady, Joseph?" All four turned in the direction of the voice. A slim woman descended the stairs, dressed in a long pale blue frock, dark hair drawn back at the nape of her neck.

"Rosie, this is my wife, and Louisa, this is Rosie. We know each other from Oak Park." Joseph had spoken without proper thought and as Louisa reached the hall, Rosie could see the astonishment in her eyes.

"Joseph, you've been gone from Oak Park nearly thirty years. I must say Rosie is wearing very well for someone you knew that long ago. I could have sworn she was about the same age as the boys." Her eyes twinkled.

"You can't be forty," Henry said, looking puzzled.

"She doesn't have to be that old," Edward mused."She might have been an infant when Pa knew her. That'd make her only a bit more than thirty." He gazed at Rosie. "You don't look thirty. You're too short for a start. And ladies of thirty don't have their hair down. And they wouldn't wear such a worn-out jacket."

Rosie was indignant. "I'm not thirty. Or forty! I'm just thirteen." She hastily shook Joseph's jacket off her shoulder and folded it over her arm, then said carefully, When Joseph – Uncle Joseph – says Oak Park, he's thinking of his sister Jane, my . . . my . . ." She trailed off. In 1900, Jane wasn't anyone's great-great-grandmother.

"Your mother!" Louise finished. "Of course. I should have guessed. But why on earth did you mention Oak Park, Joseph?"

"Oh, I suppose because Rosie looks so like Jane did at her age, when we were working there."

"You do look like Jane," Louisa said. "There's a great family likeness. And your mother told us all about you on her last visit. Of course we wanted to meet you before, but we're not that long back from Burma. And then Joseph is away so often and your parents so busy with the farm . . . " She stopped as something else occurred to her. "But I understood your name was Violet."

"Is it? I mean it is. Yes," was all Rosie could think of to say.

Edward seized on this. "If you're Violet, you're not Rosie, are you? I mean you're either one or the other. And we sent a birthday card to Violet MacDonagh. And a present. Not to Rosie MacDonagh."

Joseph answered, which was just as well since Rosie had no bright ideas on the matter.

"Of course you can be Violet and Rosie," he said. "Especially if you were christened Violet Rose. Then you can call yourself Rosie if that's what you prefer."

"Ah." Edward nodded, the mystery satisfactorily explained.

"So I hope it's a nice surprise for you to meet your cousin, Rosie MacDonagh. She's going to stay a few days – if it's no inconvenience, Louisa."

"How could it be an inconvenience, Joseph, to have your sister's child visit? But you should have told me and I'd have got Mollie to organize the guest room. You and your surprises! I bet you didn't tell the poor girl you're off to Cork tomorrow? I suppose that's a surprise too – that she won't even get to see her uncle while she's here."

Joseph groaned. "Oh no. I forgot. Rosie I am sorry. I've urgent business in Cork, otherwise I'd postpone it."

"Isn't he the terrible man, Rosie? Inviting you here and then disappearing." Since Louisa was smiling fondly at her husband, Rosie reckoned she wasn't too cross.

"Not to fret, "Loisa added. "You are most welcome and the boys will entertain you royally."

"Ma! Do we have to?" Edward was glum.

"She's a girl, Ma," explained Henry. "Girls are no fun. They like playing with dolls and they do embroidery and sewing. And they don't mind doing lessons and being neat and tidy."

Astounded, Rosie asked, "Do you know any girls?"

"Gosh no. Well, we know Amelia Smith down the road. But she says we're too rough to talk to."

"I don't play with dolls," Rosie said. "And I can't sew or embroider and I hate homework. As for being neat and tidy, Mum – Mother – says my room looks like a rubbish dump. She says I put nothing in a wardrobe or a drawer that can go on the floor. But she's always exaggerating."

"A rubbish dump!" Henry's tone was admiring.

"Can't sew or embroider!" His mother was horrified. "I'll get Mollie to show you. She's a fine needlewoman. A few hours' practice every day and you'll be a great help when you get home."

Rosie felt depressed. She hadn't travelled all this way to learn sewing. A few hours a day! Her fingers would be pin-cushions.

Seeing her glum expression, Joseph rescued her. "The child is here on a holiday, Louisa. No tasks for her. She must be allowed to enjoy herself. And if I hear another word from you two about girls, I'll get Mollie to teach *you* embroidery. Is that clear?"

"Oh Pa, you wouldn't!"

"I would. So what do you say? Are you going to entertain her?"

"Yes, Pa. We'll treat her like a boy."

Rosie was indignant. Just because she couldn't sew or keep her room tidy didn't mean she was a boy! Before she could say so, a hot-faced girl came into the hall and picking up a heavy baton swung with all her might on the gong in the alcove. The hall shuddered and each of them groaned and put their hands over their ears, pressing closely to shut out the reverberations.

"Glory be to God, Molly! You don't need to sound the gong when we're all in the hall. Couldn't you just tell us lunch is ready. Our heads are singing!"

"Sorry, sir. Cook said to make sure and give it a right clatter so you'd hear it. She says you're all deaf when it suits you. I like to do what Cook says, sir. Otherwise she gets terrible cross." And she hurried back to the kitchen.

Mollie set an extra place for Rosie in the dining-room. To begin with, lunch was a quiet affair, as Rosie took in the dazzling white linen tablecloth, the heavy silver cutlery, the sideboard crowded with china, silver framed family photographs and heavy candlesticks. Watercolours of the Killarney lakes hung on triangles of cord from a picture rail. Opposite was a mahogony fireplace, the mantlepiece teeming with ornaments, a huge mirror reflecting the rest of the room. Heavy velvet curtains framed the window. Small tables, plant stands, rugs, a chest of drawers – no space was left unfilled. Crystal chandeliers hung from the ceiling. The light bulbs looked odd, Rosie thought. Not like bulbs at all, sort of grey mesh. Joseph followed her gaze. "It's a gasolier," he said. "We have some electric lighting in the city streets, but not in many houses."

"I'm afraid you'll have to use a candle in your bedroom," Louisa added. "We have gas downstairs only."

"What about toilets? Do you have toilets?" Rosie asked, remembering the chamber-pots in Oakpark and the horrible outdoor privy in North Great George's Street that none of the sixty tenants ever used. Rosie had never given toilets a second thought until that trip, but afterwards she had never taken them for granted again.

Louisa was a bit taken aback. "We have the very latest toilet," she said proudly. "The best modern plumbing."

"Thank God!" Rosie was fervent.

"Do you have toilet problems?" Henry was interested.

"This is not a proper subject for lunchtime, Henry!" His mother glared at him and he said no more.

Lunch started with a delicious light soup. Rosie was too busy scoffing it for conversation. Suddenly a pellet of bread stung her face.

"Ouch!"

Opposite, Henry's and Edward's grins disappeared when Joseph asked, "Are you all right, Rosie?"

"Yes, thank you." She glared at the boys.

From then on, anytime their parents weren't watching, she was attacked with bread pellets, flicked by finger and thumb from across the table. There was nothing she could do but brush each pellet onto the floor, otherwise her place would look a mess. She thought of firing back a complete roll, but found the twins' mother staring at her when she raised one. She smiled, brought it back to her mouth and bit into the dry bread.

Rosie's chance for revenge came a million pellets later, when desert arrived. It was semolina pudding.

Joseph remembered some post he was expecting and slipped out to the hall to check. Louisa suddenly wanted a quick word with Cook about the evening menu. When they'd gone and before the boys could move, Rosie used the back of her dessertspoon to splatter both their faces with semolina.

When Joseph came back, she was eating politely though without enthusiasm. The semolina tasted a bit like wet gravel. The boys were still wiping their faces.

"Henry! Edward! I told you before. Food is not a weapon. It is to be eaten, not fired. Just look at the mess you've made of each other. You've semolina on your faces, on your jerseys and on the table. I'm afraid this is once too often. I think you will have to write out the chapter on 'Table Manners' from your mother's housekeeping book."

"But Pa, we didn't throw it. On our word of honour, Pa."

"It's true, Pa. Ask Rosie. Please Pa. Those chapters are twenty pages long. We won't have time to put up the flags for the queen. Tell him we didn't throw the semolina, Rosie."

"They didn't throw the semolina," Rosie said.

But before she could tell him who did, Joseph said, "Well,

all I can say is you two are the messiest eaters I've ever come across. And I don't see why poor Mollie should clear up after you. You can do it yourselves. No! I won't listen to any excuses." He held up a hand against protests. "That is my final word, do you hear?"

"Yes, Pa."

"When you're finished, I'll be in my study with your mother."

"Yes, Pa."

Joseph went off to the kitchen to explain matters.

Rosie was contrite. "I would've told him it was me," she said, "only he didn't give me a chance."

They bore no grudge."Well, at least you didn't tell him we threw the bread," Edward said.

"And you're a really good shot," said Henry. "If I tried to fire semolina with the back of a spoon I'd miss every time. It'd be all over the wall and furniture."

After that Rosie felt obliged to help them clear off the table.

Chapter 5

IN THE kitchen, having lunch were Cook and Mollie.

"Up to your tricks again, boys!" Cook sounded cross. "And who's this then?"

Rosie was introduced to Mrs Dempsey, who told her, "I'm so pleased there's a young lady here to put a bit of manners on these two. Their poor pa thinks they're sloppy eaters, but I bet they were up to something with that semolina. 'Twere never their favourite puddin' and I reckon they'd do anything with it other than eat it."

Feeling guilty, Rosie just smiled.

Mollie winked at her and said, "Terrible wasteful too.That semolina could be used for mending the back wall. 'Tis better than any cement, so 'tis. Sets real hard."

Cook turned beetroot with annoyance. "If you don't like my cooking, Mollie Sweeney, well you don't have to eat it, do you? In fact I won't bother preparing any more food for you."

Mollie was immediately sorry. "Oh Mrs D! 'Tis only your semolina I don't like. Sure you have a magic touch with everything else. You know that's true, Mrs D. But why must you make semolina that no one eats?"

She turned to the twins, "I bet your pa and ma didn't eat any. I bet it's all still in the bowl. Well, except for what you two decorated yourselves with. Amn't I right?"

The twins nodded and Mrs Dempsey looked depressed. She said quietly, "I shall get my semolina right, you wait. It won't get the better of me. I have to keep trying and one day you will be begging me for extra helpings, Mollie Sweeney!"

"Certainly I will . . . if I amn't poisoned in the meantime," muttered the maid.

Cook's face went purple this time and Rosie said hastily,"Your soup was ace, Mrs Dempsey. "She was afraid Cook might have a fit. "And your roast potatoes were deadly!"

The twins groaned. Molly gasped with shock. "You're in for it now!" she murmured.

"Deadly!" Cook rose from the kitchen table, leaning across to Rosie. She lifted a tea towel and began flicking vigorously at crumbs. She was breathing heavily. As she was a large woman, Rosie found her behaviour quite worrying, getting the distinct impression Cook wished she were a crumb.

"Deadly!" Cook's voice was choked. There was absolute silence in the kitchen.

Rosie realised her mistake and hurriedly said, "It's not an insult, Mrs D. Where I come from, people says 'deadly' for something that's really good. And your cooking is really good."

Everyone in the kitchen held their breath. Cook looked at Rosie's earnest face and stopped flicking at crumbs. Her expression cheered up and everyone began to breathe again.

"Well, I can't be gossiping with you lot," she said. "There's work to be done. You'd best get on with clearing the table."

Mollie risked a joke. "If ye don't hurry up, that semolina will set terrible hard and we'll have to chip it out of the dish!"

This time Cook smiled. A weak smile, but a smile nonetheless.

When Rosie and the twins had finished clearing up, the boys fetched their father from the study.

"The neighbours are out already, Pa. You can hear Amelia

Smith screeching. And Mister Johnston has the Union Jack flying from his window. The whole street will be done before us, Pa."

"Well, go and fetch the bunting then. It wouldn't do to be last, would it?"

The twins raced off.

"Why is everyone putting up flags?" Rosie asked.

"For Her Highness," Joseph said. When Rosie looked blank, he explained, "For Queen Victoria. The royal yacht is arriving at Kingstown next Tuesday. Her Majesty will stay on board overnight and the next day she will make a state visit to Dublin."

"Is that good?" Rosie asked. She had a vague idea that Queen Victoria did not head any popularity polls in her Irish History book.

"Most of us see her visit as an honour," Joseph said. "And April the 4th – next Wednesday – has been declared a public holiday."

"You mean people are looking forward to her visit?"

Joseph smiled. "Of course. People love a holiday. It will be marvellous, Rosie! A colourful procession of royal carriages through the city. Brass bands. A guard of honour. The royal regiments. So many lords and ladies. Everyone is looking forward to it. There are special trains from all over the country, bringing those who want to see her. It will be a glorious day, Rosie. A great day for Ireland. Thousands will line the streets to see Her Majesty."

"And everybody likes her?"

"Well. Nearly everyone. There are a few people who, it appears, would prefer not to be a part of her great empire. But they are foolish people, Rosie. They bring only trouble."

About to argue, Rosie found the conversation brought to an end when the boys arrived breathless in the hall, carrying a huge cardboard box.

Outside there were neighbours and servants in the gardens and on the avenue. Edward and Henry began twining red, white and blue bunting the length of the railings, while Joseph directed operations and chatted to neighbours. Up and down the avenue manservants were climbing ladders, fixing flags. A huge banner hung over the centre of the road. The purple lettering was clearly visible against the black background:

Welcome
Victoria Regina

Next-door a large pole extended from the upstairs window. On its flag an image of the elderly queen fluttered in the breeze.

Rosie was fascinated. Soon the avenue was a sea of flags and bunting. In a nearby garden a servant was busy setting head-and-shoulder statues on a wooden stand. "Our great generals," she heard the man say.

A manservant went back inside the house to fetch more bunting. Henry looked around to see who was watching, then looked at the ladder.

"What's your name?" A girl her own age was standing beside Rosie. She was holding a red white and blue umbrella over her head even though the sun was beaming.

"Rosie, what's yours?"

"Amelia Smith. You're staying with the O'Neills aren't you? Where are you from?"

Rosie remembered who she was supposed to be. "Meath," she said.

"Ah. And how large is your father's estate? Is it as large as Powerscourt? My father is Lord Powerscourt's second cousin, you know." The girl had an irritating drawl, as if speaking was too much of an effort.

"I'm not sure how big the farm is." Rosie was beginning to think the questions were very nosy.

"Oh, a *farm!* Your father is just a *farmer!*" Amelia's tone was one of infinite pity.

Rosie began to feel very insulted on behalf of this non-existent father. Before she could defend him, Amelia had noticed Henry high up on the ladder at a nearby lamppost. "Look at that silly boy!" She cried. Joseph, still chatting to a neighbour, turned around.

In a flash, Amelia was over at the lamppost, shaking the ladder with her free hand. "Get down at once, you stupid, stupid boy!" She was shouting, making sure everyone could hear her efforts at getting Henry to see sense. Edward stopped working on the railings.

"She's really very sly," Rosie thought,"pretending to help Henry when she just wants to get him into trouble."

Henry was doing his best to come down the ladder, but Amelia was shaking it so much, he couldn't make any progress. Rosie decided to beat the girl at her own game. "Get away from that ladder, Amelia!" she roared. "You're trying to knock him off."

Amelia stopped at once and glared at Rosie, her game ruined.

Henry climbed down at fast as he could, but not before Amelia jabbed his bottom with the umbrella.

"Ouch! That's really sore!"

"You deserve it." Joseph was beside him, seething with anger."I told you and Edward not to climb the high ladders. But of course you never listen. You were about to fall off."

"But, Pa!" Edward said. "That wasn't Henry's fault. She was pushing the ladder."

"No excuses. Inside at once, Henry, and up to your room. You too, Edward. I can't trust either of you." Fuming, he marched indoors, the twins following.

Remembering the adventurous boy she had known in Oak Park, Rosie felt disappointed in Joseph.

"He's turned into a father," she thought.

Work done, the road emptied of people as neighbours went indoors and servants cleared away ladders and boxes.

Amelia was looking at Rosie, who smiled sweetly. "That is such a nice umbrella," Rosie said. "It must have been so expensive."

"It was. Mother ordered it from Brown Thomas. It's made of silk."

"Really. It's beautiful. I'd never be able to afford one like it. Could I hold it? Please. Just for a second?"

Flattered, Amelia handed over the precious umbrella. Immediately Rosie ran down the road to the last ladder left in place. Swiftly she climbed up, hung the umbrella from the flag-line and was back down before Amelia realised what she was up to.

When she did, the girl raced down, wailing, "You rotten swine!" Her voice was no longer a drawl. "Get my umbrella at once!"

"Get it yourself," Rosie said. "Only be careful, 'cos I might shake the ladder!"

Amelia rushed off to her own house and Rosie thought it was time to disappear.

Making her way back along the empty avenue, she was lost in thought, trying to decide if she preferred the boy Joseph had been to the responsible man he had become. "I wonder will I change too?"

Opening the gate to St John's, she jumped when a heavy hand gripped her shoulder from behind. Turning, she could not help the shock and terror that registered on her face.

The eyes that looked into hers were not quite sane. They burned and glittered in a face that was twisted with hatred. A deep scar dragged the man's mouth down on one side. He was breathing heavily. She tried to twist out of his grip but it was useless.

"You better keep still," he told her, "if you don't want to get hurt." He squeezed her shoulder till she cried out. "That's just a taste," he said. "Compliments of Mr Donnelly!" He relaxed his hold slightly. When she was silent, he smiled and his face looked even more twisted. Even if she'd wanted to speak she couldn't. She was frozen with terror.

"I know you're staying with Joseph O'Neill," he said. "Now you tell him, for I don't think he believes me, that if he don't give back what's rightfully mine, then I shall come after him. And not only him, but all who belong to him. D'you hear?"

He was digging his fingers into her again, as if he were trying to dislocate her shoulder-bone and Rosie moaned with pain.

"D'you hear, girl?"

"I do," she managed.

He towered over her, his face menacing and said softly, as if to himself, "Why, I almost have a mind –"

At that moment the upstairs window opened. The twins leaned out. "Let her go!" Henry yelled. Edward chucked a heavy glass marble which hit Donnelly on the side of the head. Instantly his grip loosened and as he turned Rosie gave him a great kick and rushed past him. The door opened and Mollie pulled her in.

Donnelly was almost foaming with fury. He shook his fist and ranted, "You'll be sorry. The whole lot of you. You'll suffer! I want what's mine and I'll kill for it if I must. Tell that to Joseph O'Neill!"

For a moment his eyes gripped Rosie's, his expression frighful with rage. She shuddered, knowing he meant every word.

Then he was gone and Mollie shut the door.

Chapter 6

"DID THAT brute hurt you, Miss?"

"I'm all right. Really, I am."

"I've seen him before, when he called on Mr O'Neill. I may be only a tweenie, but I'm a tweenie that knows her manners and knows a gentleman when she sees one.And that fellow is no gentleman!"

"A 'tweenie'?" Rosie was temporarily distracted. "What's a 'tweenie'?"

"I am," Mollie said, leaving Rosie no wiser.

Joseph had just come into the hall and Mollie turned to him, "Oh, sir. That horrible man – the one with the scar – is after attacking Miss Rosie on the street. In broad daylight, sir!"

"He didn't really attack me," Rosie said, concerned at Joseph's sudden pallor. "I'm all right.'

"Sir, I think he's dangerous. He was shouting and roaring. Now I know I'm only a tweenie, sir, and it's not my place, but shouldn't we be telling the police?"

Rosie's heart sank. If the police came and questioned her for any length of time, she was bound to reveal that she did not belong to 1900. They would probably think she was mad. At the very least, it would be so embarrassing.

Joseph saw her anxiety and said, "Well, Mollie. There's no

damage done this time. But certainly if he comes near Rosie again, I will do as you say."

"It's not just Miss Rosie. He was threatening us all, sir. Even a tweenie like me."

Once again Rosie wondered what a tweenie was. Mollie's surname was Sweeney and perhaps she had difficulty saying it, but since she could pronounce all other words, that didn't seem likely.

"I promise you, Mollie, " Joseph was saying. "If he comes near us again, I shall summon the constabulary at once."

"But, sir –"

"That's my last word on the matter."

Mollie sighed, "Yes sir." Shaking her head, she went back to the kitchen.

"What's a tweenie, Joseph?"

He smiled, "It's a young maid-of-all-work. A skivvy. You remember? You were one in Oak Park, though you weren't very good at it." He paused, then said apologetically, "I'm sorry I can't spend more time with you today. I have to sort out papers for this trip to Cork. As soon as I get back, we'll have a good chat. And don't worry about Donnelly. He's made two tries now and he must realise his clues have vanished forever. He'll hardly come back again."

Rosie wasn't so sure. She was about to tell Joseph that she had what Donnelly was looking for when he said, "I really must go and finish my work. Mollie put your bag into the guest room. It's the first right on the landing. Dinner is at seven and I'm sure you could do with a rest in the meantime. I'll see you then."

The guest room was lovely, Rosie thought. The late afternoon sun warmed the polished oak floors. Comfort was added by a couple of rugs and dark blue velvet curtains. The walls did not close in like those in the dining-room, but were pale yellow. There was no clutter here. A small oak wardrobe and a washstand with jug and basin were the only furniture apart from the bed. Rosie's bag was on the floor, the old jacket folded on top of it.

The bed was cast-iron, high off the ground. The metal springs almost shrieked when Rosie flopped down. She bounced vigorously and they made a sound like skidding car-tyres. She stood on the matress and jumped up and down just to hear the noise, and was making a colossal racket when the twins peered around the door.

"We knocked," Henry said, "but you didn't hear."

"Who was that man?" Edward got to the point. "What did he want?"

"We heard you and Pa talking in the hall. We would've come down, only he told us we had to stay in our room. We heard Pa saying that man – Donnelly – wouldn't come back. He said it as if you knew who Donnelly is."

"What's going on, Rosie?"

"Please, Rosie. Tell us!"

Rosie stopped jumping. The boys looked at her eagerly. "Go on, Rosie. You don't know how boring the hols have been so far. Tell us what's going on."

"But you'd never believe me."

"We would, Rosie. We would."

She considered. "I'll tell you," she said at last, "but you must promise never to say a word to anyone else, not even Joseph –"

"And that's another thing!" Edward cried. "You always call Pa 'Joseph'. You never call him 'Uncle'. Anyone would think he was your pal!"

"We promise," Henry cut in. "Tell us your secret, Rosie."

And so she told them. Not everything. Not that Joseph was a time-traveller too. Not about his letter. She reckoned that was his business and if he wanted them to know, then he'd tell them. But she told them about her own gift. And how she'd first met their father in Oak Park and they'd become great friends. That he knew of her gift and had recognised her when she returned. Which was why he pretended she was his niece. That she'd kept a jacket belonging to him and she'd come across the clues in the sleeve. How she'd come back because she wanted to see Joseph again and that Donnelly was after the clues.

She gave them details of Joseph's life in Oak Park and she could see their round eyes change from amazement to slow belief.

"But how do you know Donnelly? Did he work in Oak Park?"

"I don't know him. But Tom Hannigan, another servant in Oak Park, knew him. Donnelly gave the clues to Tom to mind and he hid the paper in Joseph's old jacket. Don't ask me how I know that, 'cos I can't tell you."

But they were only interested in the clues.

"Clues!" Edward sighed with pleasure. "Treasure. A scarred villain. I can't believe it!"

"As good as a Sherlock Holmes mystery," Henry added. "You must show us that paper, Rosie. Go on!"

"But I have to give it to Joseph. Then he can return it to Donnelly and no one will be in danger any more."

"You can't give it to Pa!"

"Rosie, this is our chance to have a marvellous adventure."

"Besides, Donnelly doesn't deserve the treasure. After all, he's a murderer."

"Think of it, Rosie," Edward said. "All those golden sovereigns. We could buy sherbets and bulls'-eyes and model soldiers and a mechanical circus. You could have a pearl necklace, Rosie and a parrot, all exotic colours and you could teach it to curse –"

He stopped, suddenly aware that the others were staring at him.

"I don't want a parrot that curses," Rosie said. "I don't want any kind of parrot. And I'd look stupid in a pearl necklace. I think you're getting carried away. But it would be exciting to find that gold."

Swiftly she went to her rucksack, unzipped the side pocket and took out the paper, a biro and her notebook. Then all three sat on a rug. Henry fingered the plastic cover that held the clues. "Is this a new kind of glass?" he asked. "It's very odd."

"No, it's plastic. Just like this pen." She gave him the *bic*. He studied it while Edward ran a finger up and down the outside. "This can't be a pen," he said. "It's got no nib."

"And what's plastic? And why is this plastic harder than that plastic?"

"It's a material you make and you can make it hard or soft," Rosie said, sorry the subject had been brought up, since she knew nothing about it. "And you don't need a nib, because the ink is in that skinny tube and it comes out through the point – a bit like a fountain-pen."

They were fascinated. "How do you fill it?" Edward wanted to know.

"You don't," Rosie told them. "It lasts for ages and when the ink runs out you throw it away."

"Throw it away!" They were horrified. Edward seized her notebook and wrote his name on the first page. Then Henry had a go. "It's magic," he said. "How could you throw it away? It must be so expensive."

"Twenty pence," Rosie told them.

"Twenty pennies! One and eightpence!" They spoke together, "Why, a fountain-pen costs two and sixpence!"

"Does it?" Rosie was fed up with biros and fountain-pens. "Look, I brought a few of them with me. You can have one each. Do you want blue, green or red?"

They stared at her with such reverence that she groaned. "I hope you're not going to start again. I mean, they're just cheap pens. They're not gold or anything. So can we get back to looking at the clues?"

They did. But only after the boys had tried all the biros and gone on about them so much that Rosie thought she might stab them with one. In the end she gave them three each, which made them ecstatic. Then she rummaged around the rucksack and found an old marker for herself.

When she saw their dropped jaws, she told them, "If you say one thing about this marker, just one, I am taking back the clues."

Their mouths shut and they managed to restrain themselves even when she wrote her name under theirs and it was orange.

"Ready?" she grinned.

They studied the paper. The boys looked at Rosie, then back at the clues. "Do you know what these mean?" Edward asked.

"I haven't a – no, I don't. But if they'd been easy to understand, Donnelly wouldn't have given them to Tom Hannigan to mind, in case Tom got the treasure for himself."

"I think we should take them one at a time, starting with number one."

Rosie read the first clue aloud: "*Mac may not stay in the Monkstown sweet shop, but Jones must be added.* I haven't the foggiest what that means."

"Well, let's go to Monkstown and find the sweet shop. Then maybe we'll find the answer to the clue," Henry suggested.

"How will we find the answer when we don't understand the question?" Rosie grumbled.

"Have you a better idea?" And when she shook her head, they agreed to go to Monkstown the next day. Rosie hoped there weren't a dozen sweet shops.

After dinner, Rosie longed for the telly. Instead, while Louisa played the piano softly and Joseph sat in the armchair reading more of his boring papers, she had a game of checkers with Henry while Edward set out some model soldiers on the table.

They were made of lead, some like Arab horsemen, others painted in the glorious regimental colours. Edward arranged and rearranged the figures, muttering to himself all the while.

"Edward! What are you doing?" Rosie could stand it no longer.

Henry groaned, "You shouldn't have asked. Now he's going to tell you."

"Tell me what?"

Edward licked his lips. "Not many girls have an interest in military matters, Rosie," he said. "but I can see you're different. I can see you'd want to know about tactics and strategy and manoeuvres and –"

"No, I wouldn't." Already Rosie's eyes were beginning to glaze.

"This is Lord Kitchener," Edward hurried on, pointing out a model with an enormous moustache. "And these are the valiant Britishers –"

"Oh God!" Rosie tried to stifle a yawn, while Henry rested his head on the table and moaned.

"And that –" Edward pointed to the lead horseman " – that is the Khalifa Abdallah. Lord Kitchener defeated him at Omdurman and won back the Sudan for the empire. Shall I tell you how?"

"Please don't," his brother said, head still on the table. At this stage Rosie was yawning madly.

Joseph lifted his eyes. "Edward! You are *not* to relive the battle of Omdurman. Can't you see how tired Rosie is?"

"But Pa! She wants to know."

"I don't. I don't," Rosie protested.

"But you asked me." Edward looked reproachful.

"Did I? Well, I'm sorry I did, 'cos I'm not interested in battles and stuff, especially not ones that happened over a hundred years ago."

Joseph frowned, but Edward just said, "Two years ago, actually."

"You look tired," Joseph told her. "Perhaps it's time to go to bed, Rosie."

For once in her life, she agreed. Time-travel was exhausting. It was strange, but there was so much to get used to in the past, so much that was new to her.

And the episode with Donnelly had drained her.

She knew Joseph was quite wrong about the man. Donnelly had been about to do her some serious injury when the twins and Mollie came to her rescue. She was sure of that. But what was the point in telling Joseph when he was away the next day?

Donnelly wasn't sane, she thought, and therefore he was very dangerous.

And the closer they got to the treasure, the more of a threat he would become.

Chapter 7

WHEN ROSIE came down to breakfast on Thursday morning, Joseph had already gone. The boys were still at the breakfast table, but Louisa, they informed her, was in the morning-room.

"Do you have an afternoon-room and an evening-room, too? Is there a room for every part of the day?" Rosie wondered.

"No," Edward told her, "we have the small sitting-room, mostly for ourselves, and if we're having lots of visitors, we use the drawing-room. And Mother receives her friends on Thursday morning in the morning-room."

Rosie thought of home and the warm kitchen and how most visitors seemed to end up there, with a glass of wine or a cup of coffee. It was more friendly somehow than a morning-room and a drawing-room.

"I wanted to say goodbye to Joseph," she said.

"Pa told us not to disturb you. He said you were tired out travelling," Edward grinned. "I suppose one hundred years is a long journey."

"And for once, I'm glad Pa's gone," Henry said, "otherwise he'd have wanted to entertain Rosie and we'd never get to find the treasure. Let's plan exactly what we're going to do."

Edward had it all worked out. "First we tell Mother we're

going to bring Rosie out. Then we go to Monkstown, find that sweet shop, ask for someone called Mac and see why he can't stay there."

"Brilliant idea!" His brother was sarcastic. "These clues are only thirty years old and of course Mac – if there is a Mac – is bound to be still in the shop – if there is a shop!"

Edward ignored him. "Another thing we need to do," he mused, "is find Tom Hannigan."

"Why?" Rosie asked and was immediately sorry she did.

"Because the most important rule of warfare is to know your enemy. When you know your enemy, you know his weaknesses and you can use them against him. That's the way to win battles. It's part of tactics and strategy."

Rosie wondered should she kill Edward now, before he got into his stride. Seeing her narrowed eyes however, the boy went on hurriedly, "What I mean is, Tom Hannigan could tell us about Donnelly, what he's like. He's the only one who knows him."

"Brilliant idea!" Henry was still sarcastic. "Except we have no address and Monkstown is quite big, with all those new houses around the village. And now we're looking for a sweet shop, a man called Mac and a fellow called Tom Hannigan."

"You're forgetting," Edward told him, "Tom Hannigan called on Pa last week. He must have left his address, in case Pa should want to contact him. All we have to do is find it. It's probably on a piece of paper."

"Oh, brilliant!" Henry said again. "A true Sherlock Holmes. Now we're looking for a sweet shop, a man called Mac, Tom Hannigan and a piece of paper."

His brother was patient. "And the piece of paper is probably in Pa's study."

"Which we're not allowed into. Mother would kill us. And Pa is always saying not to go in when he isn't at home, in case we disturb his precious papers."

"He never said it to Rosie though. She could go in. And if Mother found her there she'd just think Rosie'd made a mistake with the rooms."

"Brilliant!" This time Henry was sincere.

"But isn't it a bit like spying?" Rosie said.

"Oh it is. It is!" Edward was very enthusiastic.

Henry said, "I think you'd make a great spy, Rosie."

She did not regard this as a compliment and was even more miffed when he added, "I mean most girls are so soppy, just like Amelia Smith. But not you!"

She turned on him fiercely. "Most girls are *not* soppy! Amelia Smith is the only one you know and she's a pain and if you say anything else bad about girls, you can forget about the treasure." Suddenly she aimed a kick at him under the table, but missed. Bewildered by her ferocity, Henry muttered an apology.

A few minutes later, Rosie was outside Joseph's study trying the handle, half wishing the door was locked. But it opened easily and swung shut behind her without a noise.

Removing the heavy glass paperweight, she rifled through the stack of pages on Joseph's desk, but didn't find what she was looking for. Nor did she find it in the press underneath. Having searched the drawers, she lifted out the top one to see if by any chance it was stuck behind. Noticing a small knob, she pressed it. A square of wood slid over to reveal a secret cubbyhole. Rummaging inside this, she found only a wad of bank-notes.

Replacing everything, Rosie was about to give up when she saw a scrap of paper stuck behind the clock on the small mantelpiece. She picked it up.

Thomas Hannigan
3 Fisherman's Row
Monkstown

She had it! Easy to remember.

She put the piece of paper back, not wanting Joseph to find out that she had gone through his private business without his permission. Even though the twins regarded her search as exciting, Rosie felt guilty. Perhaps it was because she saw Joseph more as the fourteen-year-old boy who had been her friend, and not as the father who gave out rules and punishments and who would certainly not approve of the adventure they were about to embark on.

Louisa would not allow Rosie out in Joseph's old jacket. "It is not at all respectable. It's old and tattered, and somewhat smelly. How could your mother let you bring it?"

"She doesn't know I took it with me," Rosie said truthfully.

"It doesn't surprise me. I dare say you got attached to it when you were small. Just as Edward did to an old slipper and Henry to the hat of our Burmese houseboy. However, I shall loan you one of my jackets. It may be a little big, but it is neat. Then you will look as well-groomed as the boys."

Rosie looked at the twins and pitied them. Each was wearing a heavy tweed overcoat and knickerbockers, thick woollen kneesocks, brown boots and a shirt with a very stiff collar, which seemed designed to strangle them.

Louisa made them put on their school caps and Rosie had to wear the huge flat beret. None of them was allowed to forget gloves.

The tram stop was only a short distance away, opposite the RDS. Some of the houses and buildings looked the same as in 2000, but everything else was different. The traffic was horse-drawn – carts, traps, coaches – of all different sizes. There were stone drinking-troughs for the horses at intervals along the edge of the path. Rules-of-the-road didn't exist. Vehicles came and went on both sides and in any old order. There were no traffic-lights and the habits of pedestrians were the same as one hundred years later – they dashed across the road as soon as they saw a gap.

Rosie quite liked the long skirts and short tight jackets worn by women. But their hats were another matter. "Gross!" she thought, taking in the wide brims, decorated with huge flowers, or artificial fruit, or peacock feathers. Every man, woman and child had a hat, she noticed. She saw some boys in sailor suits with hats to match. But worst of all was the Noddy-type woolly headgear, worn by small children, so long at the back that it looked like a kind of tail, with a bobbin on the end.

"That is really desperate," she murmured, as a small child, wearing a black and yellow version stood beside her, clutching her mother's hand.

"She looks like a wasp," Rosie muttered to the twins.

They glanced at the child. "She's not a she, she's a he," Edward said.

"No, she's not," Rosie was adamant. "You can see all her curls. She's got quite long hair. And anyway, she's wearing a dress!"

Edward looked at her scornfully. "Of course he is. All little boys wear dresses. When he's four he'll wear boys' clothes – and get his hair cut!"

Rosie's mouth was open. She could not stop looking at the child whose frilly dress was evident under his coat. The little boy became very uncomfortable. He got red. Then he frowned.

When he could stand it no longer, he punched her arm and said loudly, "You're very rude. Stop staring! Stop it!" He punched her again, quite hard.

His mother glanced disapprovingly at Rosie.The little boy stuck out his tongue and gave her another dig when his mother wasn't looking. Rosie yelped and glared.

The Number 7 tram came trundling up the road along its metal lines. The electric cables vibrated overhead and the bell clanged just before it came to a halt. On the front was a huge sign:

KINGSTOWN

On the side, over the windows, were two ads the length of the tram:

VAN HOUTEN'S COCOA IS THE BEST
AND GOES THE FURTHEST

and

DONNELLY'S RIBS AND BACON – ALWAYS TASTY

Not very interesting, Rosie thought.

She stepped on after the twins and turned around as if to help the small boy, then pulled his wasp-hat over his face and down past his chin, so that now he looked like a giant caterpillar.

His mother saw none of this and Rosie had fled up the stairs before the surprised child started to wail. She smiled as she heard him, and heard the mother say very crossly, "Humphrey, it serves you right. How often have I told you not to fiddle with your hat. It isn't a mask. It must stay on the top of your head!"

Upstairs was open deck and Rosie enjoyed the journey.

Everywhere there were flags and bunting. Everywhere people were working outdoors. Houses along the route were being freshly painted in Queen Victoria's honour. Grass was trimmed, windows washed, drives swept. And here and there along the roadside were scaffolding and workmen.

"They're building stands," Henry explained. "Father has paid five shilling each for us all to have a viewing seat on the stand outside Trinity College. When her Majesty's coach goes by, and the royal carriages and the guardsmen, we'll see every thing."

"It'll be a bit like the Patrick Day's parade then?" Rosie said.

"It'll be like nothing you've ever seen before," he said.

The tram passed Blackrock Park and Rosie could see the lake. A woman was wheeling a pram with huge thin wheels. A small girl – or maybe a boy – was running with a hoop and stick.

Beyond the park Rosie could see the gardens of an estate and a beautiful home. "Frascati House," the conductor called and rang the bell. He came upstairs and Henry gave him three pennies for the fares.

They got off the tram at Monkstown Church. It was midday and the small main street was quiet and sleepy. A dog shuffled to his feet and ambled away while two tabbies dozed on a widowsill. The awnings on the few shop fronts drooped like heavy eyelids. A pub and a forge showed little sign of life. They wandered slowly down the street. The nearest thing to a sweet shop was a grocer's.

"Let's ask here," Henry suggested.

"Ask what?" said Rosie.

"Ask where the nearest sweet shop is. Or even if there used to be one."

Once inside she caught her breath.

Behind a long, polished mahogony counter, a young man in a shop coat was serving a middle-aged woman. "Cloves, cinnamon, ginger," he chanted, pulling out drawers of spices. A delicious aroma filled the shop, as he spooned the powders into small paper cones and closed them with a twist.

"A pound of sugar," he murmured, "and two pounds of flour." Taking the lid off two enormous bins, he took a silver scoop and filled brown paper bags. "A half dozen apples – only the best for you, Mrs Harty – and three oranges." He went to two wooden barrels near the end of the counter and picked the fruit. "Six ounces of tea." From a large tin canister he ladled tea leaves into another bag. "And a nice joint of bacon." He looked up at the hooks over his head where sides of meat were hanging, with fly-strips in between. Carefully he made his choice, unhooked it and on a marble slab he deftly cut the order.

It was a most interesting grocery. There was sawdust on the floor, and overhead two cables ran up to a high desk at the top of the shop, where an elderly man sat, placidly smoking a pipe. On the dark wooden shelves were an assortment of glass jars, with various pickled goods. A huge tin of mustard powder stood next to bottles of port and wine. And when the lady asked for half a pound of butter, the young man went to another marble slab, lifted a muslin cloth and Rosie saw the biggest mound of butter she'd ever seen in her life. Seizing two grooved pieces of wood with handles, he lifted a chunk of butter, set it on a piece of thin white paper and weighed it. "Seven and a half ounces," he said. "Too much?"

"That'll do," the lady said, whereupon he seized the pieces of wood, shaped the butter into a ridged square and wrapped it in the paper.

He wrote down the price for everything with a pencil, totted it up and said, "One pound seventeen and sixpence-halfpenny, Mrs Harty."

Mrs Harty handed him two banknotes and he put them with the bill into a small brass cylinder, attached it to the overhead wire and sent it skimming up the shop to the high desk. The old man came to life, caught the cylinder, emptied its contents and sent the change whirring back, all in a matter of seconds.

Rosie longed to have a go and thought she wouldn't mind spending all day whizzing that cylinder up and down the shop.

"There you are, Ma'am. Two shillings and five-pence-halfpenny."

By the time the customer had left, the boys were dying of boredom and half lying across the counter.

"Now, young lady and gents, what can I do for you?"

"We're looking for Fisherman's Row," Rosie said.

"Ah. It's down towards the sea." He gave them directions and added, "Those cottages won't be there for much longer. Due to be demolished, they are. Nice modern houses will be put in their place."

"We were looking for a sweet shop too. Is there one in the village?" Edward asked.

"No, there isn't. But if it's sweets you want, we have a selection of lollipops and fruit sherbets."

They shook their heads, disappointed.

"Do you know a man called Mac?" Rosie asked.

He thought. Then, "I'm afraid not."

They slumped, depressed. If they couldn't even solve the first clue, what hope had they of finding the gold?

The young man felt sorry for them and called up to the elderly gent, "Mr Sweeney, where's the nearest sweet shop?"

The elderly gent puffed on his pipe, got off his seat and came down to them. "Why, it must be at least a mile away," he said. "We haven't had one in the village for nearly thirty years. If you want directions –"

"No, we don't, thank you." The twins and Rosie looked at each other, hopes rising and Edward said, "So, there definitely was a sweet shop in Monkstown thirty years ago?"

"There was. It belonged to a fellow called . . . let me see now . . . I should be able to remember . . ."

"Was he a fellow called 'Mac?'?" Rosie did her best to help.

"Mac? No . . . not Mac exactly . . . I know! It was called MacArthur's, after the old man who ran the place. Then when he died his son sold the premises. It's a draper's now."

"MacArthur!" Rosie breathed. "Oh thank you, thank you. That's a great help."

Outside the shop, the boys turned to her. "How is it a great help?" They were mystified.

"Take the Mac out of MacArthur and what are we left with?" Rosie said.

"We're left with Arthur," they spoke together, not cheering up at all and Henry said glumly, "We might be left with Arthur, but we're not left with any gold. The mystery is deeper than ever."

Rosie refused to be downhearted. "'Arthur' is the answer to the first clue," she said. "And we have to solve five of them before we'll get the gold. But think of it! We actually cracked the first one."

"What d'you mean, 'cracked'? It's not an egg." Henry said.

But Edward saw her point. "Rosie is right," he said. "It *is* something to be pleased about. It's like a jigsaw with five pieces. We won't see the whole picture till we put all the pieces together."

"That's it exactly," Rosie said admiringly.

Unfortunately Edward got carried away. "See, it's just like a battle-plan. There are different parts you have to put together, to get a complete strategy. That's the way to whack the enemy."

"You'll get whacked in a minute, if you keep on about battles!" Henry was fed up.

His brother protested, "But Rosie is interested, aren't you?"

"I am not," Rosie was definite. "You keep saying that and you're wrong. Battles are boring! "

Edward went into a sulk. The other two were very relieved, so he quickly gave it up.

They followed the young grocer's directions and soon found the narrow lane that was Fisherman's Row.

Chapter 8

"IT'S WONDERFUL!" Rosie caught her breath at the tiny thatched cottages and the cobbles winding downwards, the sea in the near distance.

"It's horrible," Edward said. "Not at all modern. They've no gaslight, Rosie, only candles."

"But that's beautiful," Rosie said.

"No, it's not," Henry told her. "You don't get any proper light with candles, and you have to bring one with you when you move and they go out with the slightest draught. Besides, those cottages have no running water and no toilets. Don't you get the smell, Rosie?"

Rosie had been wondering about that. As they went farther down the lane, the pong got stronger and more awful. She tried to stop breathing.

"It's the night-soil," Edward said. He was holding his nose. "They empty their chamber-pots at the back lane and when there's a big heap, it's taken away by collectors."

"By collectors?" For a moment Rosie misunderstood. "People collect this stuff? Like antiques?"

Who on earth could be mad enough?

"No!" Edward was taken aback. "You are silly, Rosie. Like antiques! Would anybody put that stuff on their mantlepiece?"

He took a sudden fit of laughing and it was left to Henry to explain, "Some men come around with a cart and take it away, Rosie. They work for the council."

She was about to ask what they did with it, then decided she really didn't want to know.

Number 3 was at the other end of the row. As they made their way, Rosie began to see that the lane was very poor. A few ragged barefoot children stared as they passed. One of the cottage doors was open, revealing in the dimness peeling walls and a bare dirty floor. Outside, the whitewash was often grey and flaking. What had looked picturesque from a distance became rundown and seedy on closer inspection. Remembering Tom Hannigan in 1870 as a proud, strong man who had kept everything in perfect order, Rosie wondered how he'd ended up in Fisherman's Row.

Number 3 was, if possible, worse than the other cottages, the door unpainted for years and the window frames rotting.

The woman who answered their knock was middle-aged and careworn. The shawl wrapped around her thin shoulders didn't hide her shabby dress. She stared at them, unspeaking.

"Does Mr Tom Hannigan live here?" Edward asked.

"Who wants to know?" The words were weary.

"I'm Edward O'Neill," he said, "and this is my brother, Henry. Our father knows Mr Hannigan. This is our cousin, Rosie."

"And why do you want to see Mr Hannigan?"

"To ask him about a man called Donnelly."

She started and her face paled. "We've had enough trouble!" Her voice was no longer weary, but shrill with anger and anxiety. "And my brother Tom is not well. I don't want him worried, which he will be if he hears any mention of that man!"

She was closing the door and Henry put a hand out, "Oh please. It's very important. We might be able to help. Donnelly threatened Pa as well."

The woman pushed his hand away but before she could shut the door, a man's voice stopped her, "Ella, let them in. I wouldn't have any harm come to Joseph O'Neill."

Silently she stepped back and waved them into a room off the tiny porch.

Tom Hannigan was sitting in an ancient armchair, blankets tucked around him, facing an iron bed with a bare worn-out matress. The tiny grate was empty. An old picture of Our Lady hung on the damp wall. There were no other furnishings.

Rosie would never have recognised Tom. He was like an old man, shrunken and sick.

He looked at the two boys. "So you're Joseph's sons. Your father is a fine man." He turned to Rosie. She held her breath. It would be very awkward if he recognised her. In Oak Park he had taken her for one of the Brannigan children who lived on the estate. It would be difficult to explain why she looked no different after thirty years. But he didn't know her.

"I heard you say you might be able to help. What did you mean?"

Rosie looked at the woman and Tom said, "Leave us for a few minutes, Ella. I think the young lady wants some private talk."

"Does she indeed!" The woman sniffed. "Well, it better not put you into a tizzy, or she'll have me to answer to. I'll be in the scullery if you want me."

When she'd left, Rosie came straight to the point, "We've found the clues Donnelly wants," she said and was immediately sorry she'd been so direct.

Tom Hannigan's eyes rounded and he had trouble catching his breath. He started to cough – a harsh racking sound – and his eyes streamed, then bulged. He could not stop coughing and began to struggle to his feet. Rosie had a sudden awful feeling that he might collapse. The twins went to either side of the armchair and lifted him up straight. Edward patted his back. The coughing turned to a wheeze as he managed to gulp in mouthfuls of air. Gradually his breathing became more normal and the boys helped him sit back into the chair.

"Such a turn!" he said when he was able. "Lucky our Ella didn't hear me."

"I'm sorry," Rosie said. "I shouldn't have told you out straight."

"You remind me of someone," he said. "What's your name?"

She reddened and Edward said quickly, "Rose Violet MacDonagh. She's our cousin."

"Jane's daughter," Tom said. "That explains it. You remind me of her. I think." He still looked puzzled.

"Anyway, we don't think Donnelly deserves to have the clues," Henry said.

Tom agreed, "He doesn't, but I see no other way. The man's a maniac. If you don't hand over the clues soon, he'll kill us all."

A sudden thought struck Rosie and made her shiver. "But if we do give him the paper, he might kill us anyway, because we might tell the police and because the four of us and Joseph are the only ones who know he's after the treasure."

They digested this in silence. Then Edward said, "Surely he wouldn't try to murder five people. I mean, he'd never get away with it."

"But from what Tom says, he's mad enough to try," Rosie answered.

"She's right, " Tom nodded. "He's evil and insane. Let me tell you exactly what he's done already to get his hands on those clues."

He paused to gather his thoughts, then started:

"It isn't a nice tale. All those years ago, a Mr James Jones, an Irish gentleman, won a thousand sovereigns in a gambling house when he was in London on business. Mr Jones was eccentric. He didn't trust banks and he loved riddles. So when he came home, instead of depositing the gold in a bank, he hid the sovereigns and devised a set of clues to show their whereabouts should anything happen to him.

Donnelly had heard about his win and one night he broke into the man's home, demanding the treasure. Jones would not say where it was hidden, and in a fit of fury Donnelly battered him to death. Raging because he was empty-handed, the villain looked in the man's pocket-book, hoping at least to find some bank-notes. What he found were the clues, and knew immediately what they would lead to. But what he didn't know was that an old manservant had seen him commit the murder.

Donnelly thought he had his leisure to find the gold. But once he'd left the house the elderly servant raised the alarm and gave Donnelly's description to the police. The blackguard went on the run.

I knew nothing of this when he turned up at Oak Park. He'd never been a friend, but I remembered him from the old Fenian days and he gave me the clues and a cock-and-bull story with them. He hoped the matter would die down and then he'd be back. Instead he was caught and put in prison. But he never told the police about the clues."

"Why didn't the servant tell them?"

"The servant thought what he'd taken from the pocket-book were bank-notes. Donnelly went along with that."

"You could have told them, Tom."

"I wanted no truck with the law. They knew my Fenian sympathies. They'd have believed I was in it with Donnelly. Anyway, what point was there in telling them about clues that were missing?" He looked at them in sudden puzzlement. "How did you find the clues?"

Rosie had sworn the boys to secrecy about her time-travel,

so they didn't know what to say. It was Rosie herself who answered, "Joseph's old jacket turned up," she said.

"When? I talked to him last week, and he said he hadn't seen it in thirty years."

"Well, he came across it yesterday," Rosie said, leaving out that he hadn't recognised it.

Henry added, "But he had to go away on business. So he couldn't come here himself."

"Well, you just be careful of Donnelly," Tom said. "He's a mighty dangerous man."

Then Edward asked, "Is there any time when he's not so dangerous. I mean, does he have any weakness."

Tom pondered. "He has one. He cannot hold his drink. If he takes a drop, he can get careless, relax his guard. It happened once when he was on a mission for the Fenians. Four fine men were caught because of his drinking and he was never trusted again."

"And that's all you know?" Edward said, thinking this wasn't much good. Donnelly was hardly likely to drink when he was concentrating on getting a fortune. But there was nothing else.

Soon Ella came to tell them they must leave Tom to rest. At the door, Rosie turned to her, curious. "What happened to Tom? Why is he so ill?"

Ella sighed. "He wasn't always like this. When he was young he was a fine man. Strong and straight. But he caught consumption. Our father died of it and Tom probably got it from him."

"Is there no cure?" Rosie asked.

"Oh aye! If Tom were rich and could spend his time somewhere like Switzerland, well, his lungs might recover. And if they didn't, at least his breathing would be easier. But how's that going to happen, ey?"

The afternoon had grown chilly and the lane was empty. Under the grey sky, doorways were shadowy and windows dark. A sudden cool breeze made them shiver.

Rosie heard footsteps on the cobbles behind, but when she turned there was no one. A few minutes later she turned again and had a sense of sudden movement, a blur, almost unnoticeable, of someone stepping into a doorway. But when she stared all was stillness.

With a sense of foreboding she started hurrying. The lane she had thought so quaint and picturesque was suddenly menacing. There were too many alleyways and too many shadows where someone of ill intent could hide, waiting for the right moment.

The boys, lost in daydreams, suddenly found they were moving very fast to keep up.

"What's wrong, Rosie?" Edward cried. "Why on earth are we running?"

She shook her head and would not answer till they had reached the top of the lane and there were trams and people and noise and she felt safe – for a moment. Turning around, she pointed and gasped, "*Look!*"

Donnelly had stepped out into the middle of the lane, making sure they could see him. He stared at them, his eyes hooded and dead. They stared back, paralysed. But only for a moment.

The noise of an approaching tram galvanised them. With one accord they rushed across the road, barely willing to take their place in the queue. When the tram halted they clambered on board and up the stairs, praying it would move on quickly. They strained to see if Donnelly had caught up on them.

He was standing at the top of the lane now.

"*Move! Move!*" They willed the tram to go on. With a sigh of relief they heard the clang of the bell and the shunt of the wheels.

But Donnelly made no attempt to cross the road.

As the tram moved at last, his eyes locked onto theirs until it disappeared into the distance.

"We got away from him," Henry sounded triumphant and sat back, relaxed.

But Rosie wasn't so sure. "I think he let us get away."

"Why did he bother following us then?" Henry said.

"To scare us," Edward shivered. "He must have followed us from home, but we never saw him until he wanted us to. He's letting us know he could be there anytime."

They were silent, frightened at the idea.

"Do you think he knows we've got the clues?" Henry said at last.

Rosie shook her head. "No. He would've attacked us, tried to get us to hand them over. And he wasn't in that shop. He must've waited outside. He probably thought we were buying sweets or asking directions to Tom's house."

Edward mused, "He must wonder why we went to see Tom."

Again they were silent, realising there was no way Donnelly would see their visit as unconnected to the treasure. He must be quite curious to know what they'd talked about. So why hadn't he tried to find out? They couldn't figure it out.

Chapter 9

MOLLIE OPENED the front door and told them, "Heaven help you! You're in desperate trouble. Your poor mother is going to kill you!"

They looked at her blankly, dragging their thoughts back from Donnelly.

"Lord God!" Molly went on. "You fellows have no idea of the trouble you bring. And there you are now, leading your cousin astray as well. You're a bad example to her, so y'are."

The twins began to get worried. "What have we done?" Henry asked.

"Whatever it is, I bet it's your fault," Edward told his brother loyally, and added, "It usually is."

"No, it isn't!" Henry was indignant. "It wasn't me who locked Amelia Smith in the shed for three hours."

"That was a mistake." Edward was pained at the reminder. "I didn't know she was in there. At least I never ran off with her doll's pram! You looked very silly racing down the road with it!"

Henry nearly choked. "Not half as silly as you looked sitting in it, your great big feet dangling out. You'd like to forget that bit, wouldn't you?"

"How could I forget it?" Edward was aggrieved. "You crashed me into a lamppost and left me stuck in that stupid pram while you ran away. I wasn't able to get out. I will never forget Amelia Smith's face when she found me. And now –"

"Would you listen to the two of you!" Mollie said. "This has nothing to do with Amelia Smith. What time is it?"

"Pardon?"

"The time! 'Tis a pair of galoots you are!"

"Time? Oh no!" Realisation dawned on Henry. "We missed lunch."

"Exactly. And you told no one you'd not be here. Your poor mother is up the walls with worry. Three hours late you are." Mollie sniffed with satisfaction, "She'll murder you. She'll make you stay in for the whole holidays. You probably won't get to see Her Majesty. 'Twill be a terrible blow to the poor lady. Comin' all this way from her fine palace and the O'Neill twins not there to greet her. Ah yes! 'Tis a sad day."

Mollie rocked back on her heels, obviously enjoying herself.

Just then Louisa came down the stairs and the boys paled. Her face was tense and her voice stern. "Edward, Henry! Where on earth were you? Up to one of your pranks, I suppose. I'm very angry with you!"

They were about to explain miserably how they'd completely forgotten the time when Rosie rushed in. "It's all my fault. There's so much to explore here. Everything is new and exciting. I wanted to see as much as I could. We didn't get into any mischief."

Louisa's face softened. "Well, I suppose it is very different to the countryside in Meath. And I do want you to enjoy yourself, Rosie." She turned to her sons. "But it's very thoughtless of you two not to say when you'd be back. You mustn't do that again. Now go and apologise to Cook. She was very upset when you didn't turn up for lunch. Especially as she wanted you to try her improved semolina. But all isn't lost. I insisted she keep some for you. So you may eat it now."

The boys groaned as their mother collected the afternoon post and went back upstairs.

"Cook will murder you!" Mollie said, her tone hopeful. "She's in one of her rages over you missing lunch. Oh yes. She's going to roast you!" She grinned. "But only after she's poisoned you first with her semolina."

Cook had experimented with her semolina, adding so much cochineal that it was deep red in colour, though it still had the texture of wet cement.

The three ate a bowl each while Cook stood over them. Mollie tried hard not to laugh at their expressions. She had to stuff the hem of her apron in her mouth to stifle her merriment. Tears came to her eyes. Tears came to Rosie's eyes too and for a different reason. She was having difficulty swallowing the horrible stuff. It was like trying to eat a dish of thick blood.

"Do you like that now?" Cook asked her. Rosie managed a smile, her mouth like a vampire's. "Oh it's . . . it's . . ." She caught Mollie's eye. The maid had to turn away so she wouldn't laugh outright.

"It's special!" Rosie said at last.

"That's right," Edward seized on the word. "It *is* special. It's specially special. Really. *Super special,*"

He was overdoing it, Rosie thought and kicked him under the table. Mollie was wiping an eye with the corner of her apron and giving an odd snort.

Henry looked at her. "I bet Mollie would love a dish of this super special semolina, wouldn't you?"

Mollie stopped laughing. Cook looked at her, waiting for an answer.

"I'm not hungry. Not a bit. I'd get sick if I ate anything . . ." She trailed off, noticing Cook's frown, then said hurriedly, "Of course now, I wouldn't get sick if I ate your lovely semolina, Cook. That's not what I meant at all. Sure I'd love a bowl."

They watched with satisfaction as Mollie ate. Every so often she smiled at Cook and glared at the others.

They had finished and were able to sit back saying, "It's wonderful, isn't it, Mollie?"

And when Cook was out of earshot, Henry whispered, "Just like warm blood, isn't it?"

Mollie gagged.

Dinner was early because Louisa was going to the theatre with friends. She dressed for the occasion, in a blue silk skirt, with matching jacket over a delicate white blouse. Her dark hair was pinned up. Rosie watched with interest as she secured a smart hat with a bodkin. Set at a jaunty angle, it suited her and Rosie thought she looked beautiful. As she drew on her gloves, the doorbell rang and Mollie told her the carriage had arrived.

The twins and Rosie came out to see her off.

It was twilight and the lamplighter was doing his rounds. The gaslights were pale as yet, but Rosie thought they made the evening magical. The coachman helped Louisa into the carriage and her friends called out a greeting to the twins.

"Mother, can we wait up?" Edward asked. "Please. You can tell us about the play."

She smiled and nodded, "But only because it's the holidays!"

"What on earth could the second clue mean?" Rosie said a little later. They were in the sitting-room, where Mollie had drawn the curtains and lit the fire, grumbling goodnaturedly over the trick they'd played earlier. Rosie could not wait for her to leave so they could study the paper.

"At least the first clue gave us a place to go to," she said, "but this is too difficult. "*The foreign photographer with Lawrence is Bob who?*'" She read. "Can you make any sense of that?"

Henry pointed to a family portrait on the wall."That photograph was taken in Lawrence's," he said. "It's a studio in Sackville Street. It's very well known. Mother says Mr Lawrence is an artist with the camera. Did you never hear of him, Rosie?"

"How could I? He's not around in my day." They looked again at the clue.

"A lot of people work for Mr Lawrence," Edward said. "One of them could be foreign. Though whoever heard of a foreigner called 'Bob'? We'd best ask tomorrow."

"A trip to town!" Henry was delighted. "That's A one! And Mother won't object. She wants Rosie to see the sights."

"Town must be so different to 2000," Rosie said.

"Tell us what your life is like," Henry said. "Are there flying machines instead of trams?

Can people travel through time? We read about it in *The Time Machine* by HG Wells? There must be so many inventions. Tell us about them, Rosie!

Edward, caught up in Henry's excitement was on to his favourite topic. "Have there been any famous battles? War must be so exciting in the future. There must be smashing weapons!" His eyes grew round and carried away by his imagination, he asked, "And invasions from outer space? Mr Wells wrote a book about that too. Henry's right. You must tell us what it's like in your time, Rosie. Please!"

So many questions. But it was Edward's desire to know about battles that jolted her heart. Her knowledge of history was fuzzy, but everyone in her time had heard about the two world wars and the atom bombs and the concentration camps. Everyone knew that millions had died.

Edward thought of war as a brave adventure, a chance to be a hero.

"1914-18," her History teacher had made them learn the dates. "Sixty thousand young men killed in the Battle of the Somme. And that was just one battle."

How could she say that to Edward?

A dreadful thought struck her. Mum had never mentioned Henry and Edward. She had never known about them. Somewhere along the years Joseph had vanished from family records, and his twin boys might as well not have existed. When Rosie went home, she would have no knowledge of them beyond 1900.

Why was there no record?

Had something awful happened to them in the Great War?

"Go on, Rosie. Tell us."

Looking at their eager faces, she chose her words with care. She told them about aeroplanes and rockets and how men had walked on the moon and how people travelled all over the world and there were no horses on the roads anymore and no trams, only thousands of cars and buses and huge trucks. And nobody had invaded from outer space but there were lots of movies about aliens. She explained about TV and computers and the games you could play on them. Their eyes grew wider and their mouths opened, as if drinking in every word.

And no, she said, there were no time-machines. No one else in 2000, as far as she knew, could journey to the past or to the future, though some Americans believed that one day science would be able to bring the dead back to life. They made sure to be deep-frozen after death, 'cos you could only revive a body. A skeleton or ashes wouldn't do.

"Ugh!" Henry said. "Imagine coming back from the dead. That is disgusting. And you'd have to have died from something – some disease or heart attack. Imagine if half your insides were rotted away from some horrible sickness. Could they bring you back then?"

"Or if you'd been hanged for an awful crime and your relatives had you deep-frozen. Could they bring you back then?"

"They don't do hangings in 2000." Rosie felt a bit sick. The gaslamps flickered palely and the firelight cast shadows in the room.

"I expect –" Edward was at his most lofty "– if scientists could bring you back from the dead, they'd be able to cure whatever diseases you had. And I expect they'd cure your breathing if you'd been hanged. And make new insides for you if you needed them. Isn't that right, Rosie?"

Rosie nodded, unwilling to follow this conversation any further.

"And what about wars?" Edward had not forgotten.

"I've brought stuff back from 2000, "Rosie was eager to change the subject. "Sweets and that. Wait there and I'll get them."

She left the room before Edward could protest. She had forgotten to take a candle and the stairs were lit only by the pale gas lamp in the hall. Her head was full of hanged criminals and wasted bodies. The gloomy light and creaking steps panicked her. She noticed a shadow moving with her and for a moment imagined Donnelly was following. She could see his scarred face and huge hands and closed her eyes in fright. A touch on her shoulder made her rigid.

"Rosie, you forgot the candle." It was Henry. Sweet relief flowed through her. She could almost have kissed him. Instead she turned, took the holder and gave him a brilliant smile.

Within minutes she was back in the sitting-room, sharing the booty.

"Oh, smashing!" They sighed with satisfaction and munched their way through the chunky Kit-Kats and the Mars bars. "Why are they called Mars?" Henry wanted to know.

"Because they're out of this world," Rosie told them.

They looked at her earnestly. "Are they from Mars then? You said men went to the moon. Did they go to Mars too?"

She giggled and tried to explain, but already they were

distracted. Henry was eating crisps while Edward didn't know what to make of the dry pot noodles. "Mmm! These are scrummy!" Henry told her.

"Please excuse me," Edward said, spitting the pot noodles into the fire and throwing the pot in as well, "but these are worse than Cook's semolina."

"You have to add hot water!" Rosie said. "Then they're delicious." She opened a can of coke and offered it to Edward. The can hissed at him and he was startled. Holding it gingerly, he stared at the opening as if something live were inside.

"It's fizzy," Rosie said.

Edward took a gulp, rolled the liquid around his mouth, swallowed and gasped, "It's smashing!"

Henry opened the other can, mesmerised by the ring-pull and the release of air. When they had finished, they were fascinated to find they could scrunch the cans with one hand.

Later Edward took the wrappings and the empty coke cans upstairs to keep with their other treasures. "Just so we never forget," he told Rosie solemnly.

They put more coal on the fire until the flames were high, and pulling in their armchairs, the boys told her about their schooldays, about freezing classrooms and Latin and Greek and rugger and cricket and masters who were kind and those who were over-fond of the strap.

Beatings were an everyday part of school life. "But Gregson goes too far. Johnny Smith's hands were cut and swollen for a week! Gregson has coins glued to one side of the strap and he makes sure to hit with that side. He whacked Johnny Smith nine times on each hand! And all because he missed his Latin vocab. Gregson is a bully."

The boys brooded for a moment. Then Henry asked wistfully, "Is everything much nicer in 2000, Rosie?"

"It's different," she said. "Nobody's hit in school anymore."

Amazed, Edward said, "No beatings? Why, Rosie, class must be wonderful."

"Do you think so?" She was unconvinced. "Homework definitely isn't wonderful. And there's too many rules. Still, Mr Murray's deadly!" She told them all about her form-tutor and her class, and about the computer room and the language lab and the new gym.

"Paradise!" they sighed with envy.

It was nearly midnight when they heard the horses trotting down the road and the coachman's order, "Ho there! Stop."

Mollie had already opened the front door as the coachman set down the step from the carriage. Louisa chatted for a moment with her friends and Rosie memorised the scene. The carriage, the elegant woman, the coachman standing respectfully to one side were framed in the street-light like figures in an old painting. Then Louisa said her goodbyes and stepped out of the frame, coming towards them.

"Oh, Ma'am, I have supper waiting for you." It was Mollie who spoke first, sounding breathless. "Cook's gone to bed this hour and she left me in charge, only she said there'd be hell to pay if you're not satisfied, Ma'am. Sure she said there'll be skin and hair flying in the morning." Then, as if there might be any misunderstanding, "Me own skin and hair, she means, Ma'am." She giggled and unable to stop talking she went on, "'Twould be an interesting sight, Ma'am. Me skin flyin' in one direction and me hair maybe in another."

"I'm sure supper will be fine," Louisa said.

Rosie wondered if Mollie had been on her own in the kitchen all evening.

Once in the sitting-room, Louisa stretched like a cat in the armchair. "The play was marvellous," she told them.

Henry sat on the rug at her feet, Edward on the arm of her chair.

"Tell us, Mother."

"Trilby." Louisa was dreamy. "Set in Paris. Very sad. And quite eerie."

She paused for effect and Edward nudged her, "Go on, Mother."

But at that moment the door was flung open and Mollie came clattering in with supper.

Noisily she set down a huge tray, talking non-stop. "Tea-pot, cups, saucers, cream, milk and sugar. No, no sugar. Drat! Biscuits, fruitcake and semolina pudding. No, no semolina pudding. That's just my little joke, Master Henry. Here y'are." She dragged a small table over beside them and set out the supper. "I'll get the sugar now," she said.

"And bring in a cup for yourself," Louisa said. "You've had a long day."

"Oh, Ma'am. I couldn't do that, Ma'am. Cook would kill me for gross impertinence so she would. She says I'm full of it."

"Mother's going to tell us the story of Trilby," Henry said.

"I'll stop so. When I get the sugar."

But she did not bring in an extra cup and nor would she take anything from the plate she had set out so carefully. Instead she sat at the bigger table away from the rest of them and listened respectfully and avidly.

Louisa began:

"Trilby is a young girl, living in Paris. She falls under the spell of a man with strange powers. He is an Eastern European called Svengali, a musician. He looks evil, eyes staring and cruel. Trilby is hypnotised by him and he trains her voice. She becomes a famous singer. But she can only sing when he is present. He must be nearby always. He is her creator and he controls her. He makes her work so hard, always driving her. Her voice is so beautiful it charms anyone who hears it.

But then Svengali dies and Trilby's voice dies too. Her

fame disappears. No one can help her. Her friends try, but without Svengali she cannot exist. She cannot eat or drink and life has no interest for her. In the end she too dies."

"God almighty, Ma'am! 'Tis a strange sort of story. Not cheerful at all, " Mollie said.

"Well, I'd much rather *The Pirates of Penzance*," said Edward. "There was some good fighting in that."

"Was Svengali evil?" Henry asked.

"He frightened Trilby," his mother said, "and she was fascinated by him. Mr Beerbohm Tree played Svengali and he was magnificent. He certainly looked evil."

"He must've been," Rosie said. "The way he wanted to control her. She shouldn't have let him. Nobody should scare you like that. It's not fair."

Some time later in her bedroom, she wouldn't draw the curtains, preferring not to have total darkness. And she left the candle lit until its flickering shadows made her imagine shapes in every corner and she had to blow it out.

She thought of Donnelly. He wanted to terrify them. She thought of his scarred face and dead eyes, of his threats and how she'd imagined he was on the staircase following her. And as she thought about him, a small flame of anger began to burn steadily. They would sort Donnelly out, somehow. He was not going to frighten her. She would not let him.

Chapter 10

BUT FRIDAY morning brought new terrors, when Henry was kidnapped.

They were waiting for the tram to town when it happened. All three had spent a restless night and were up early. It was Henry who decided they should waste no time. "If we get an early tram we'll avoid the nine o'clock rush to work and we'll be there when Lawrence's opens."

There was no one else around when they saw a horse and trap come flying up the road. They could hear the crack of the whip and see the animal's eyes rolling as it galloped at full speed. Only at the last minute, when it was almost on top of them, was the horse pulled up with great strength. It shuddered to a halt. They had time to notice the animal's straining muscles and the sheen of sweat, and then Donnelly leaned over and hoisted Henry into the cart, one hand holding the boy in front of him like an awkward parcel, the other cracking the whip and shaking the reins. The horse shot off again and Donnelly roared back, "Wait there. D'you hear. Wait there!"

They waited for an hour and a half, trying to come to terms with the fact that Donnelly had kidnapped Henry and that he intended no good. At first they thought to tell Louisa, or the police. "But if he sees her or a policeman, he won't come near us," Rosie said. So they stayed, while the rush-hour came and went.

At ten Donnelly came sauntering up the street. "You wouldn't listen, would you?" He was grinning at them. "Well, now you'll have to. I've got your brother and you won't see him again 'less I get those clues. So you go and tell your pa that. Tell him he has till midday. Tell him to meet me here with what's mine. Otherwise his boy is dead!" He drew a finger across his throat, stared at them and walked away.

"Why wouldn't you let me give him the clues?" Rosie cried. She had been about to take them from her pocket and hand them over, but Edward had gripped her arm hard and shaken his head. Now the opportunity was gone.

"He doesn't deserve them," Edward said, watching Donnelly.

"Henry doesn't deserve to die," Rosie was sharp.

"He won't die. This is an adventure Rosie. Henry loves adventures."

"Don't be daft! This isn't a *Boys' Own* story. How would you like to be kidnapped by a murderer? I must say it's not very nice, leaving your brother in the clutches of a maniac! It's not very nice leaving your twin unrescued when you could swop him for a piece of paper!"

Donnelly was in the far distance now, but still visible.

"We *are* going to rescue him." Edward's eyes were narrow. "Do you think you could follow Donnelly without being seen?"

"I could try. What have you in mind?"

"He's turning up towards Donnybrook. Pa thinks he's living somewhere in Ranelagh. You follow him, Rosie, and if you find out where he's staying, meet me at the tennis club as soon as you can."

"Why don't you come with me? What are you going to do?"

"There's no time to tell you. Donnelly might get away."

Rosie rushed in the direction the villain had taken. Around by the Dodder, past the library. It was only when she was at the bridge in Donnybrook that she saw the man turn up Eglinton Road. She followed, keeping in by the railings, the overhanging trees screening her from sight.

He looked back only once and Rosie darted into a garden. Donnelly made for Ranelagh village and Rosie hurried to keep up with his long stride. He disappeared up a side road near the Chester Dairy and then turned down a narrow lane. It took her some moments to figure out his route and when she saw him again he was outside a shed, turning the key in a huge padlock. Rosie stood behind the corner wall until he had gone in, then as silently as possible she crept up to the door. She could hear Donnelly's voice but not his words and she pushed the door in a little.

"You and me got another hour to wait, boy. And if I don't get that paper you're a gonner, see!" The words were plain now and they were followed by a groan and a muffled choking noise. Donnelly laughed. "No point you trying to talk. All trussed up like a turkey waiting for Christmas, ain't you?"

A filthy skylight in the sloping roof allowed a faint light to filter through. The shed was filled with junk. Old iron bedsteads and bits of furniture. Peering around the door she could make out two shapes in the gloom at the back. She pushed the door a little too far forward and a line of light shot across the floor. Rosie darted back and when she heard Donnelly grunt his way forward, she raced for the corner.

When he looked out there was no one there. "Must've been the breeze," she heard him mutter. All the same he took the padlock and chain in and she could hear its rattle as he locked the door on the other side.

Rosie sped back to the village, asked directions for the

tennis courts and was waiting only a few minutes when she saw Edward and three boys running towards her.

"Donnelly has Henry locked in a shed up a lane," Rosie was still gasping. "There's a load of junk and Henry's tied up at the back. And there's a skylight."

She looked at the boys. One of them was her own age, the other two about ten and eight. As a rescue party they didn't look very impressive.

"These are the Nelligans – George, Bernard and Samuel. School pals. They live nearby. Now. I'm going to think of a plan."

"Well, you'd better hurry up 'cos your brother is choking in there. And Donnelly is coming down to your house at midday. I think he expects Joseph to hand over the clues."

"Right." Edward frowned in fierce concentration and muttered, "Strategy. Tactics. That's what's needed."

Then his face cleared. "Right!" he said. "Rosie, you hammer on the door. That'll distract Donnelly. We'll get in the skylight when he's opened up. Then we'll grab Henry and rush past him."

"You'll have a hard time. Henry's trussed up. Like a turkey, Donnelly said. I can't see you getting him out over all that junk."

Samuel, the smallest boy, began to empty the pocket of his jacket. He took out twine, a small catapult, marbles, a toy soldier and finally a penknife. "We can use this." He offered it to Edward.

"Smashing. Samuel, you stay with Rosie. Give her a hand." Edward pulled out the blade and slipped it into his own pocket. "Ready?"

They crept up the lane, Samuel murmuring once, "This is very exciting!"

The other three climbed the wall beside the shed. One by one they hoisted themselves onto the roof. George dislodged a loose brick from the wall and they held their breath. Nothing happened.

Rosie seized the brick and as the boys edged towards the skylight she used it to batter on the door. Samuel used his steel-tipped boots. Then she motioned him to stop and shouted, "Mr Donnelly! Mr Donnelly! I've a message from Joseph O'Neill!" She heard a noise on the roof and hammered again, this time roaring, "Mr O'Neill says it's urgent!"

She stepped back and looked up. The boys on the roof were tugging in vain at the skylight. It was stiff after years of disuse.

She whispered to Sam who had his ear against the door, "Donnelly better not open up yet."

But it was too late. The chain rattled and the door moved a chink. Rosie banged again, this time roaring with all her might, "Thanks for opening the door, Mr Donnelly."

The boys on the roof took the hint and the sound of breaking glass was masked by the din at the door and the now fierce rattle of chains. They dropped down. George made for Donnelly, the others for Henry.

"You trollop you!" Donnelly was snarling. "Are you trying to wake the dead? This better be worth while."

He was not prepared for what happened next. Before he could yank the door back, Samuel sank his teeth into his fingers. The man howled and shook his hand free. Rosie flung the brick on his foot and launched herself forward. Donnelly staggered back, reeling.

George in the meantime had found a cache of tin kettles and teapots and began flinging them at the villain. They made a hollow ringing sound against his head.

Bernard and Edward had cut through the ropes tying Henry and were busy releasing him.

He gurgled and moaned behind the gag until one of them thought to untie it. Henry gasped and vomited.

"That filthy smelly rag," he groaned and vomited again.

Edward lifted the gag to his nose, "Yeuch! The thing smells like horse dung and Brussels sprouts mixed together."

Henry was trying to rub some life back into his numbed arms and legs, but there was no time. Gripped by the other two, he stumbled towards the light. Meanwhile George was flinging everything he could lift at Donnelly, as Rosie and Sam cleared an escape route through the junk.

Donnelly couldn't figure out what was happening. The shed seemed to be filled with people. How had they got there? One way or another he would stop them getting the boy out. But he had no chance when Sam found a trolley and shoved it across the floor. Donnelly's knees buckled on impact. He sat down on the spout of a kettle. The pain was terrible but this was not the worst.

As he lay there moaning and trying to gather his wits, three sturdy boys ran over his body, their boots on his stomach pumping the air out of him. He opened his mouth to gasp and found the filthy smelly gag stuffed into it.

"Serves you right," Edward told him.

Then they were gone. All of them.

They stopped running when they got to Ranelagh village.

"You're good pals," Henry told the Nelligans. "Thanks for helping."

"That was great fun," Samuel said, then added wistfully, "I don't suppose there's anyone else you'd like rescued?"

"Not today, Sam. Thanks all the same," Edward said. "You three better run like hell. Donnelly will be after us."

A tram had stopped nearby and he turned to Rosie and Henry. "Let's go into Sackville Street like we planned."

Safely on the Number 11, they had the satisfaction of seeing Donnelly emerge from the lane and stare up and down the village, his expression raging and frustrated. The

Nelligans had disappeared and it was only when the tram had shunted by him and gathered speed that he looked up and saw them on the open top. He practically danced up and down, shaking his fist. They waved back, grinning.

"Goodbye, Mr Donnelly."

"Hope you have a sore head!" Edward roared.

"And a sore belly!" Henry shouted.

"And a very sore bum!" screeched Rosie.

The boys thought this was the best and all three chanted at the furious villain, "Sore bum! Sore bum! Sore bum!" until Donnelly was out of sight.

Luckily there was no one else upstairs to disturb with their yelling. By the time the conductor arrived to see what the commotion was all about, they had collapsed into giggles.

But Donnelly the clown had once again become Donnelly the terrifying villain by the time they reached town. For Henry told them how he'd been treated.

"I think he might've killed me," he said. "He kept clipping me around the head and saying he'd teach Pa to ignore him. He was in a rage and said if he could trick Pa into giving him the clues without having to hand me over, he'd do that. The man is twisted. He blames Pa for being in prison. I told him it wasn't Pa who'd murdered someone and anyway he hadn't even heard of Donnelly till just recently. It wasn't his fault the clues were hidden in his jacket. But Donnelly wouldn't listen to reason. He just kept hitting me and telling me to 'shut it'. Said he wouldn't be at all surprised if Pa had put his filthy hands on the gold years ago. He was tying the rope really tight and shoving that smelly cloth into my mouth and asking me how Pa could be such a toff now and live so well when all he'd been thirty years ago was a poor orphan servant boy.

He kept prodding me for an answer, but I couldn't give

one, could I, with that gag? All the time he was getting madder and saying why should Pa have everything while he had nothing. And maybe he wouldn't wait, but kill me anyhow. That's when you and Sam started clattering on the door, Rosie. If you lot hadn't turned up –"

Henry swallowed, his face deathly pale and they were silent at the thought of what might have happened.

Then Rosie said, "But we did turn up. And we beat Donnelly."

"We did, didn't we?" Henry began to cheer up.

Town was dressed up for the coming occasion. Lines of Venetian masts, streamers and flags stretched from College Green right up to the Parnell Monument. Messages to Her Highness were everywhere on banners. There was no sign of any litter, though the visit was still days away. Fresh paint glinted in the sunlight, new awnings shaded the shops, windows were polished, paths swept and washed. Nelson on his pillar smiled down on all the red, white and blue of what looked to Rosie like a very British city.

"It's weird!" She remembered this same street in 1920, full of violence and hatred for the Black and Tans. Now Portraits of Victoria were on every second lamppost, and the banners proclaimed a huge welcome to *Our Empress and Our Gracious Majesty*.

Did most Irish people feel British in 1900?

Getting off the tram they were distracted by a slight scuffle. A young man bearing posters had been stopped by two policemen who were well over six foot, their spiked helmets making them even taller. With little bother they wrested the posters from the grasp of the young man.

"Now you go on your way, sir. We want no misery-louts trying to ruin people's happiness. 'sTis a time for celebration."

"Celebration!" The young man was red with annoyance.

"We have been robbed of our liberty. People *should* be miserable!"

"Well, if you persist with these notices, sir, you can be miserable all on your own down at the station. There's a nice little miserable cell just waiting for the likes of miserable you."

A few onlookers had gathered. "Shame on you!" one woman told the young man, who muttered and moved away.

The two policemen smiled, shook their heads and threw the posters in a bin. When they'd gone, Rosie took some out. She read:

UNITED IRISH LEAGUE

DEMONSTRATION AGAINST ROYAL VISIT

WED 3RD APRIL

AT NOON

IN SLANE COUNTY MEATH

Another advertised a torchlight procession through Grafton Street on the night of the Queen's visit, again in protest. And a third was for a *Rival and Giant Children's Party*, on the same date, to be held in the Phoenix Park. A wonderful event, the poster promised, not to be missed by patriotic children. It was being organised by *Maud Gonne MacBride and her assistants*.

"Is the Queen giving a party for children?" Rosie asked, trying to imagine the lady in the portraits playing musical chairs and pass the parcel.

"Well, she won't actually be there. It's in the Phoenix park on Wednesday," Edward told her.

Henry added, "I bet she'd have a good time. Pa says old ladies don't have energy for children's parties. But she'll be sitting in that carriage for hours. It'd be nice for her to have ice cream and jelly and chocolate and fudge and –"

"We should have kept her some pot noodles, " Rosie said. Henry was making her hungry.

"Or we could bring her some of Cook's semolina-slab," Edward said. "Except she won't be there. So could we stop talking about it? Let's go into Lawrences."

He pointed out the shop at 7 Upper Sackville Street and they darted across the wide road, dodging horses and carts and carriage traffic.

The sign in the window proclaimed:

WILLIAM LAWRENCE.

Photographic Studio. Toy Bazaar. Fancy Goods.

On the ground floor was the toy department. A clockwork carousel was operating on a pedestal. It was breathtaking, painted in reds and yellows, the toy horses and riders moving up and down and round and round, while carnival music tinkled.

There were other clockwork figures – an organ grinder with a monkey on his shoulder, a drummer boy ready with his sticks and drum, a fellow with a drink half-lifted to his mouth. These had not been wound up and Rosie was dying to see them in action. And she would have loved to investigate the old-fashioned scooters and huge spinning tops and the boxes of board games, the beautiful porcelain dolls that sat on the shelves along with the Jack-in-the-Boxes and the *Magician's Chest of Deceptions*. She was in an Aladdin's cave from the past and she wanted to spend some time there.

"Come on, Rosie. We have to go home soon. The studio is upstairs."

In a daze, she followed the boys, to find herself in a long gallery of framed photographs. There were pictures of people, of scenery, of buildings and monuments. There were shelves of photo-postcards with views from all over Ireland. There were albums of all sizes and there were miniatures on ivory of Queen Victoria. In fact one whole wall was given over to pictures of the queen, all for sale. She was very dumpy, Rosie thought. And old. And very cross-looking.

Rosie was curious. "Are those photos selling?" She asked the gentleman behind the mahogany counter.

He looked at her over his half-moon spectacles. "Of course they sell," he said. "They sell like hot cakes, Miss. A lot of young ladies particularly request a portrait of Her Majesty to hang on their bedchamber walls."

Rosie looked again at the photos. "She's like a pop star then." She spoke without thinking.

The gentleman raised his eyebrows. "There is no connection between Her Majesty and a bottle of lemonade or indeed the stars."

She looked at him, baffled, and he stared back wondering would he ever understand modern youngsters.

Edward leaned across the counter and got to the point. "Please, can you tell us? Did a foreigner called Bob ever work here?"

"He did not. No foreigner has been employed on these premises."

They looked at each other, hopes fading.

"Never? Not even in1870?"

"Never!" He was exasperated.

"Are you sure?" Rosie didn't want to give up.

He looked at her icily, "Young lady, I am certain. And you may take my word for it since I own the premises." He was quite cross now and went on, "And we've never had a 'Bob' either, unless you count Mr Robert French, our esteemed photographer. But to my certain knowledge, not once in all his years with Lawrences has he been called Bob. Nor is he foreign!"

The three looked at him gloomily. Then Rosie began to smile.

"French is foreign," she said simply, "and Robert is Bob!"

The man behind the counter began to get red in the face, but before he could say anything the boys began to jump up and down. "That's it, Rosie. You have it! Yippee! The answer is 'French'!"

Had there been any room they would have tried a somersault.

A young man who'd been waiting patiently stepped forward. "Excuse me, Mr Lawrence, I've come to collect a portrait." He handed over a docket.

The man glanced at the docket and rose, "Just wait here a moment, Mr Pearse, while I fetch it."

Henry and Edward were already bounding down the stairs, but Rosie was stopped in her tracks.

Was this Patrick Pearse? Staring at his profile she thought he did look like the photo she had in her schoolbook, though it was of an older man. He turned and smiled politely at her, then Mr Lawrence came back with the portrait, checking the details of the docket: "Portrait of yourself, Mr Patrick Pearse, and of Mr Willie Pearse." The young man nodded.

Rosie gasped. It was him!

Portrait wrapped, he went down the stairs, Rosie following. Near the door another young man waited, "Ready, Patrick?" He folded the newspaper he'd been reading and waved it. "Lord, Patrick, even *The Freeman's Journal* is full of the Queen's visit."

"You could say the same for the Irish people, Willie. All they seem to be interested in is having a holiday and a party." He shook his head gloomily, "It'll take us another century to get freedom at this rate. And no one to care." He caught Rosie listening and smiled, "What do you think, young lady?"

Afterwards she was raging with herself. She could have

told him as much as she knew of what lay ahead. She could've told him about 1916. Or at the very least have said how different things would be in a hundred years' time. Instead she blushed with shyness and was unable to speak. She stood there awkwardly as he and his brother left the shop.

And when at last she came out onto Sackville Street, they were gone.

Henry and Edward were waiting impatiently. "What on earth kept you, Rosie?" But they weren't interested in the answer.

"What about this second clue?" Edward went on. Neither of them were as thrilled as they'd been in the shop. "We have Arthur and French, but what does that tell us? Nothing!"

Henry was equally depressed, "We're no nearer solving the riddle. It just gets more confusing."

"We *are* nearer," Rosie said. "We're two clues nearer."

When they didn't cheer up, her heart sank. "You're not thinking of giving up, are you?"

"Don't be daft, Rosie," Edward told her. "After all, Lord Kitchener won't beat the Boers in a day. War takes time."

Rosie didn't know what he was talking about. She wasn't going to ask either.

"This is the best Easter holidays I've ever had," Henry said. "If you weren't here, Rosie, Mother would have us at our studies, or going with her on her visits. We just sit there saying nothing while she chats with her friends for hours. Or else she makes us dance. So of course we're not going to give up."

She laughed. "If you think getting kidnapped by a maniac is better than your usual Easter holidays, you must have had some rotten times."

"We have!" They were fervent.

She was about to ask them what dancing they had to do when Edward said, "Aren't you enjoying it too, Rosie?"

She didn't have to think. "It's much more interesting than watching telly or helping out with the housework!"

"Housework!" The looks they gave her were suddenly concerned. "Are you very poor, Rosie?" Edward's voice was sympathetic.

Rosie thought of Mum, always going on about how lucky they were, not to want for anything, when there were so many people living in poverty.

"No. We're not poor. Why d'you ask?"

"You do the housework. That's the maid's job. And if you don't have a maid you can't have much money," Edward explained.

Rosie considered. None of her friends' parents had maids, but they all had cars and machines and they weren't poor.

"I don't think there are any maids in 2000," she told them.

They looked at her with great sympathy. And Henry added, "Your holidays must be even worse than ours. We never have to do any cleaning or polishing. Well, except as a punishment. You can't have made much progress in a hundred years if there are no maids."

Grumpily, she said, "I s'pose maids must be happy not to be maids any more. I s'pose that's progress. For them anyway." But she couldn't help feeling very envious all the same.

Chapter 11

AT HOME, there was a letter for each of them from Joseph. Rosie took hers to her room.

Dear Rosie,

I am looking forward to seeing you next week and am sorry not to be able to spend more time in your company. Although the Cork office is very busy, you have been much on my mind these last few days.

I started remembering our talks in Oak Park about time-travel. It was our opinion that the gift could only be used when a relative from the past needed our help. And of course it occurred to me then why you've come back. You think I am in some danger from Donnelly.

You may have got the impression from me that Donnelly is no real threat, and he isn't as far as I am concerned, for I can take care of myself. But he is a danger to someone of your age, since he is somewhat unhinged. But mad as he is, he is bound to realise sooner or later that his clues are not going to turn up after thirty years. Then he will give up. If he hasn't done so by the time I return, I shall ask the police to deal with him.

In the meantime, Rosie, please be careful and have nothing to do with him. Just have a good time with the twins.

There is as much excitement here over Her Majesty's visit as there is in Dublin, with many people travelling to see her. Cork may well be empty on the day with all the extra trains the GSR are running.

I have written to Louisa and the boys (not about time-travel, of course – they would think me insane) and shall see you all on Tuesday evening.

With fond regards,

Your Great-Great-Uncle Joseph.

It was odd, Rosie thought. In his other letter he'd signed off as Joseph. Now he was her great-great-uncle.

"We have to solve the clues before Tuesday evening," Rosie told the boys. They had finished their dinner and were in the sitting-room. "Joseph says he'll get Donnelly arrested when he comes home."

Edward made a face. "That means it will all come out about the clues."

"Yes. And Donnelly knows for sure now we have them. He'd tell the police rather than let us get to the treasure. Then they'd take over."

"Righteo, "Henry said. "Let's solve the third one tomorrow. We can't do anything on Sunday. Mother always takes us out. So that leaves two days for the last two clues. It could be a bit of a rush."

His brother was more confident. "Of course we can do it," he said. "We've managed a clue a day so far, plus rescuing a nitwit from a lunatic – ouch!" He doubled up in mock pain as Henry jabbed him.

"Why am I a nitwit?" Henry demanded.

"Because," Edward said piously, "you don't listen to your mother. She's always telling you not to stand at the edge of the kerb. Of course she just thought you might fall under a tram or a carriage. She didn't realise you'd be picked up like a parcel by Donnelly. He couldn't have done that to Rosie or me, 'cos we were standing well back. But you might as well have had a big sign on you, saying *Please Kidnap Me*. That's why you're a nitwit and me and Rosie are really clever – ouch!"

This time Henry had kicked him.

The twins wrestled on the floor, then settled down to playing with Edward's toy soldiers.

Rosie took up the *Irish Times*, pretending to be deeply interested. She did not want any lectures on battles.

The front page was just ads. The news was inside. There were no photographs. The small tight print looked very boring. Three long pages were about the Boer War and the rest of the paper was given over to Her Majesty's visit.

In spite of herself, Rosie started reading:

The Royal Yacht, escorted by ships of the fleet, will arrive in Kingstown on Tuesday evening, the third of April, at six o'clock. On arrival a salute will be fired. Her Majesty will remain on board overnight.

Next morning Her Majesty will travel in the company of Princess Christian of Schleswig-Holstein through the capital to the Vice-Regal Lodge in the Phoenix Park. The King's Dragoon Guards will escort the royal carriage, which will be followed by the Earl of Denbigh, the Countess of Antrim, the Duchess of Connacht as well as the prince and princesses.

Streets will be lined with troops and there will be bands along the route as well as many viewing stands for loyal subjects.

Boys from various schools and brigades will be drawn up at the entrance to the Vice-Regal Lodge to welcome Her Majesty. A military review of three thousand will follow.

Rehearsals for the above will take place in the Fifteen Acres on Sunday afternoon.

Members of the public are requested to be at their viewing places early on Wednesday, as no strolling will be permitted for three quarters of an hour before and after Her Majesty's carriage and procession have passed.

No vehicles will be allowed into the city between 7 pm and midnight, which will allow the public to enjoy both the illuminations and the firework display.

Suddenly Rosie was looking forward to Wednesday. It was going to be one huge party, she thought. Why wasn't it mentioned in her History Book?

In Glasnevin cemetery, beneath the divided elm, find the last word on Battling Henry.

Rosie read the third clue out to the boys after breakfast next day.

"We can't get out till this afternoon," Henry told her. "Mother wants us to deliver invitation cards. She's decided to have a musical evening."

"When?"

"Tonight." Henry was glum.

"Which means we have to dance," Edward said, his face tortured.

"Oh good." Rosie had no sympathy. "That should be a laugh."

"You won't be laughing when Mother asks you to sing!"

Rosie's face changed. "She wouldn't!"

"She asks everyone to do something," Henry said. "No. That's not exactly true. She *insists*."

"Oh God. But I have a desperate voice. I'm not allowed sing in school."

"Are you not?" Edward was genuinely interested. "You must sound awful. Let's hear."

"No, I won't." Rosie changed the subject. "Hurry up and deliver those cards. Then we can get off to the cemetery."

When they were gone, Rosie decided to listen to her CD player in her room. No one would hear it if she used the earphones. She had just taken it from her rucksack when there was a knock on the door. Hastily she put the player into the pocket of her jacket on the bed and stuffed the earphones under the pillow.

Louisa came in, looking a bit hesitant. "Rosie," she said, "I hope you don't mind my mentioning this, but I've noticed you haven't changed your dress since you got here."

Rosie went beetroot. Did Louisa think she wasn't bothering to change her clothes? She couldn't say she'd only brought lots of knickers. Louisa would think she was weird. Any of her other clothes would look very odd in 1900.

"I hope I haven't upset you, Rosie. I expect some mistake occurred over the packing. She looked pointedly at the rucksack that Rosie had left in the middle of the floor. "I'm sure your mother organised a suitcase and you forgot to take it."

Rosie was mortified.

"Well, I shall send Mollie to you with one of my dresses and some underclothes, if you have no objection. The dress will need some alteration, but Mollie is a skilful needlewoman. She will be sure to make you look pretty for tonight."

"Thanks. Thanks very much." Rosie was scarlet. She knew Louisa meant well and she'd have been even more embarrassed tonight wearing the grubby clothes she had on her. But she didn't like being thought scatty enough to forget her clothes!

Mollie made her stand still as she pinned up the hem of Louisa's blue dress.

"You're the lucky one," she said, pins gripped in her teeth. "Sure this dress almost fits you except for the length."

Rosie sniffed.

"Aren't you the right eejit all the same, Miss Rosie," she went on,"forgettin' your suitcase and you coming on a holiday? And I bet you have lovely garments at home."

"I have." Stuck in a Victorian dress, Rosie thought longingly of her own clothes. Forgetting herself, she got carried away. "I have palazzos and flairs and chinos and tee-shirts and sweatshirts and denims. I've gone off Docs though. Definitely not cool. I wear Addidas or Nike and –"

"Will you hold on a minute!" Mollie looked bewildered. "I can't follow one word. Are you talking foreign? Because if you are, Miss, it isn't kind! All I wanted to know was the kind of dresses you wear. No need for smartness."

"I'm sorry. I don't have any dresses." Seeing Mollie's look of disbelief, she hurried on, "I have skirts." She wondered what the maid would think of her two minis. Mischievously she said, "D'you think skirts and dresses will ever get shorter? D'you think they'd ever be this length?" she pointed to a few inches above her knee.

Mollie spluttered and a couple of pins shot out of her mouth. "Glory Be! What sort of scandalous female would wear such items? 'Tis bad enough the way some show their ankles without any regard for being respectable. But no female could dress in the likes of what you're saying. Sure they'd have to be hauled around in a bathing-box! And God knows the bathing-costume is shocking enough!"

At this stage Mollie was spluttering pins from her mouth in great numbers. Rosie decided against asking what she'd think of bikinis.

Chapter 12

THE AFTERNOON was grey and misty. A slight drizzle was falling by the time they reached the cemetery.

They had seen no sign of Donnelly, but he had followed them, waiting till the last second to get on the tram, staying downstairs near the platform, hidden by parcels and bags and old-fashioned buggies. When they got off near the cemetery, he waited till the next stop, then hurried back in time to see them pass through the massive iron gates. They were sauntering, certain that for some reason he had missed them.

Raging at their successful rescue, he had half decided on a revenge attack once they reached the trees along the avenue. It would be easy enough to take them by surprise and bundle them undercover. Then he would teach them. They couldn't get away with how they'd treated him! A good hiding would give them some respect.

He studied the avenue and saw that if he slipped behind the trees he could get ahead and cut them off farther up.

Moving under cover, he was just alongside them when they stopped. He saw a gardener pushing a wheelbarrow and cursed.

"Excuse me, please," Rosie said. "Could you tell us where 'the divided elm' is?"

"'The divided elm'?" The gardener scratched his chin. "I'm afraid I – oh, wait a second. There's a huge elm tree that was split by lightning years ago. Is that the one you mean? It's still growing, mind you. Quite a sight too. Like two trees in one."

He gave them directions. Impatiently, Edward rushed ahead. The other two were more leisurely. After all, this should not take long and they had all afternoon.

Under the trees, Donnelly stood lost in thought. The girl had told him yesterday at the warehouse that she had the clues, but he hadn't believed her. Now he knew it was true. Why else would she ask the gardener such a peculiar question?

"Why did that fool Joseph hand over the clues to her?" he pondered. "Maybe he's lettin' those kids do his dirty work for him," was the only answer he arrived at.

He followed, curious now to see what they were up to. Wanting to hear what they might be saying, he hurried to catch up.

In a remote corner, overgrown with shrubs and trees, the elm tree towered. Its branches reached like huge twisted arms towards the grey sky, leaves touching across the V of the colossal trunk. The mist was thicker in this neglected place, swirling around the mossy gravestones.

As they crunched along the gravel, the old tree seemed to reach towards them as if in warning. Rosie stopped. So too did Donnelly, his feet slipping on the grass so that he scrambled to keep his balance.

"Did you hear that?" Rosie looked around, but could see nothing in the mist.

"Probably Edward," Henry said. "There's only us – and the leaves rustling and the trees creaking."

He made it sound like the loneliest place on earth.

"And there's a lot of dead bodies," he added conversationally. "They don't stay still you know. It is a scientific fact, Rosie. You see, the soil underneath the coffin moves every so often and then the bones groan and creak. It's because they're disturbed."

"They're not the only ones who are disturbed," Rosie muttered. He was giving her the shivers.

Just then they heard a low moaning sound.

"Oh, God!" Rosie clutched Henry's arm.

"Not to worry," he said. "It's only the dead turning in their graves."

He was very calm, she thought.

"*Whoooooh Whoooooooooooooh!*" Edward jumped up from behind a gravestone.

"*Aaaagh!* Oh no, oh no! Henry. Oh God, it's a ghost. We're dead!" Rosie nearly died of fright.

The ghost was clutching her arm, very firmly for a spirit. And he was laughing which wasn't very ghost-like. When she realised it was Edward she attempted to strangle him, but she couldn't as he still had a grip on her arm. After a few moments she calmed down. "You two!" she said in disgust. They grinned at her and she had to smile back.

"There's the grave we're looking for," Edward pointed. It was right underneath the elm tree. They crouched to read the inscription, scraping at the moss with their fingernails.

Battling Henry Butler
Born 1834.
Died 1869.
A noble pugilist
R.I.P.

Underneath was a short verse:

Here lies Battling Henry
Who fought with grit and zest
Until laid low in round nineteen
By a hammer-blow to his chest.

Edward stated the obvious. "The last word is 'chest'."

"So what have we got now?" Henry pondered. "We've got Jones, Arthur, French and Chest."

"And none of it makes any sense at all," Edward was depressed. "I mean, what has Battling Henry's chest to do with hidden gold? Still, maybe you're right, Rosie, and when we find the rest of the clues, everything will be clear."

Nearby, Donnelly caught the words 'chest' and 'clues'. "So they do have them! And they're after a treasure-chest. Maybe it's here."

But the three had turned back the way they'd come. Absorbed in their own thoughts they never saw the figure in the trees. His eyes glinted. "Think they'll take what's mine, do they? I'll get those clues before they leave this cemetery!"

They ambled along, trying to fit the pieces together and not succeeding. It wasn't difficult for Donnelly to reach the gates before them, to swing them shut and hide once more.

Hearing the clang of iron, they looked up. "My God!" Rosie whispered. "We're locked in."

About to hurry forward, they stopped dead. A heavy figure stepped out from a tree near the entrance. The mist was a shroud around him and for a moment Rosie thought he was one of Henry's moving dead. Then he made towards them, hands outstretched, and they shrieked.

Rosie was the first to recognise him, but when she turned to tell the others they were gone. They had disappeared into the shrubbery. She would have tried to escape too but was frozen with fear. The idea of being trapped alone with Donnelly paralysed her.

He stopped moving forwards, enjoying the fact that she was terrified. He laughed. "On your own, 'ey? No guts those boys. Useless!"

Rosie caught a glimpse of movement in the undergrowth and knew she was not alone. The twins were ready to help should Donnelly attack. But they had no weapons this time and the element of surprise had been with their enemy.

"Right!" he snarled. "If you know what's good for you, you'll hand over those clues now!"

He shouted the last word and Rosie jumped, immediately putting a hand in her jacket pocket. The paper was there. So was her CD player. She took a deep breath. She hadn't a clue what disc Dad had left in it. She prayed for one of his terrible tracks. It might at least distract Donnelly and give her some time.

With her thumb she found the 'play' button and pressed. Silence. Raising the volume to its highest, she waited.

"I warned you. I want those clues." The hulking figure moved towards her and at that moment the sound began.

What on earth was it? Not for the first time she thought her dad had the wierdest taste. Then she recognised it. It was from *Best Film Soundtracks* and it was *Psycho*.

Donnelly was rooted. Shuddering, he looked left, right and behind, head almost swivelling. His hands flailed as if he were trying to clear the mist.

The music was from the murder scene and the sound was frightening, tense.

"Zing! Zing! Zing! Zing!" Violin strings plucked on raw nerves.

Donnelly could not shut the sound out. He howled and ran without any sense of direction, past Rosie, crashing through the gravestones.

She pressed the 'off' button and turned to call to the boys, but they weren't there any more. Puzzled, she moved to the gate.

She heard them first, urging each other to hurry. Then she saw them, clambering up the great iron gate.

"Hi," Rosie sauntered over. "Donnelly's gone. It's safe now."

"No, it's not!" Edward gasped. "Didn't you hear that awful sound? Like music from hell. It's the dead haunting us. Hurry! Take my hand. I'll pull you up. Quick. *Please Rosie!*"

Instead she leaned against the gate and said, "D'you mean this?" And she started the player again. Almost at once she switched it off as they nearly fell off the gate with fright. Then they pulled themselves to the top. Rosie pushed at the other side which swung open. "It's not locked," she said, and sauntered through.

When the twins were standing beside her, she took out the CD player. "The awful sound was this. Listen. It's only a machine. Now don't get a fright."

They found it hard to stay. If Rosie hadn't been so calm they'd have taken to their heels. When the track was finished and she'd switched it off again, Henry said, "That is horrible. How can people like that kind of music in your day?"

"They don't, not exactly. This was used for a scary film." She explained about the movies, but they knew a bit already.

"Oh, moving pictures," Edward said. "They have them in America. Mother thinks they'll never catch on."

"Yes, they will." Rosie was definite.

On the way home in the tram, Henry asked to see the CD player. Then he pressed the button and *Psycho* started again. Loud and eerie, waves of sound crashed through the upstairs which was three quarters full.

Passengers jumped. One or two gave a scream. As the music got more tense, fear mounted. People clutched the strangers beside them and moaned. They looked around wild-eyed and seeing nothing, two, then three, got up and dashed downstairs. A moment's hesitation and the rest followed.

The bell clanged again and again as frightened passengers signalled the driver to stop. As soon as he did they tumbled off the tram.

Those below who hadn't heard the music thought only a

fire could cause such panic. They too jumped up and jostled their way past the conductor who was collecting fares. Within minutes he was alone, wondering what the emergency was.

He rushed upstairs to find three youngsters collapsed in laughter. "What did you do?" he asked. "What did you do to those people?"

"We didn't go near them," Edward managed.

"Then why did they rush off the tram?"

Rosie stopped laughing long enough to say, "They were hearing things. They were hearing weird music! An orchestra."

"An orchestra! Where would we get an orchestra on a tram? It's against the rules to play instuments. It disturbs the peace." He paused, looking at them through narrowed eyes. "Were you three playing instuments?"

"No," they said earnestly, then roared laughing again.

And since he could see no sign on them of any instrument he gave up. Wagging a finger he told them, "If I find out any different, there'll be trouble, d'you hear me? A lot of trouble!"

But he was talking to himself. The three were rocking on their seats, wiping their eyes, too convulsed to hear.

All the guests had arrived to Louisa's musical evening by eight o'clock.

There was the elderly gentleman who clasped his hands together at the end of every turn and said, "Beautiful! *So* beautiful." Rosie wasn't at all surprised to hear he was totally deaf. There was a middle-aged couple with a son in his twenties. And the last to arrive were Amelia Smith and her mother, both dressed in pink and white satin, reminding Rosie of two ice-cream cones.

Louisa played a piano piece from Chopin. It went on a bit long, Rosie thought. But it wasn't half as long as the old gentleman's song. He quavered on and on about his lost love who'd died so young. "Probably from listening to him singing," Rosie muttered to the twins who took a fit of sniggers.

The middle-aged wife whispered that she had a sore throat and was unable to sing. Without thinking, Rosie clapped, and the old gentleman immediately said, "Beautiful! *So* beautiful." The twins had to put their hands over their mouths to stop laughing.

The middle-aged husband recited a poem called "Khubla Khan". It sounded great, Rosie thought, though she didn't understand one word.

Then their son sang "The Bunion that Blossoms upon my Big Toe". This was much better than lost loves and Rosie listened carefully.

There's a bunion that blossoms upon my big toe
And that bunion resembles an onion and lo!
To dance I'm unable
For my feet are unstable
And my bunion it bothers me so
Yes! – My bunion it bothers me so!

Well, it wasn't Oasis, but it was the best so far. Not for the first time Rosie wondered why people in the past went in for this kind of entertainment. Except it wasn't really entertainment. More like torture. And when Amelia Smith screeched out, "I'm only a Bird in a Gilded Cage", Rosie wondered was everyone else in the room suffering too. Apparently not, for the old man clasped his hands and said, "Beautiful. *So* beautiful." And Mrs Smith called for an encore.

"Oh please! *Don't!*" Rosie said under her breath.

But she did.

"Have you ever heard anything like my Amelia?" Mrs Smith asked the guests.

"No. Never!" Rosie was certain.

Mrs Smith beamed at the compliment and told her, "My

Amelia will further her studies at the *Conservatoire* in Paris. What do you think of that?"

As an answer was expected Rosie said fervently, "Well, I definitely think she should study somewhere. And Paris is nice and far away."

Beside her the boys made a choking sound, but Mrs Smith just beamed again.

Then Louisa called on Rosie to sing.

"No, please, " Rosie said. "You don't want to hear my voice. It upsets people. It's much worse than Amelia's – I mean – it's not as good as Amelia's."

But Louisa wouldn't listen. "You're being very modest. I'm sure you have a beautiful voice."

"No, I haven't."

In school the choir-teacher had nearly wept when Rosie sang "Down by the Salley Gardens". She'd compared the sound to long sharp fingernails scraping across a blackboard. "So please," she'd told Rosie before asking her to leave the choir, "do the world a favour and don't ever sing again in public."

But if people in the past wouldn't listen, they had only themselves to blame.

The twins were egging her on, in spite of what she'd told them earlier. "Go on, Rosie." Edward said, "You'll be smashing!"

"A1!" Henry added.

After Amelia's performance she was tempted to sing "When the Going Gets Tough the Tough Get Going", but knew from her visit to 1920 that people in the past didn't understand this kind of song. So she decided on one David Byrne had taught her, called "There Once was a Girl". It was a bit mad, about an insane girl who had murdered her whole family, but it was the only one she knew that told a story. People from the past seemed to like stories.

Rosie coughed and started:

There once was a girl who wasn't nice
Her family had to pay the price
For she did each one of them in – in – in ñin
She did each one of them in.

She gave her mother cyanide
And her mother as she died
She smiled a hideous grin – grin – grin – grin
She smiled a hideous grin

She pushed her father in the creek
The water was poisoned for a week
And so they did with gin ñgin ñgin – gin
And so they did with gin.

At this stage Louisa faltered on the piano. "Probably having trouble with the tune," Rosie thought. The middle-aged couple seemed to be in pain and their son had his head in his hands. Mrs Smith and Amelia were in some sort of hypnotic state, eyes staring, mouths wide open. Rosie was miffed, "It's not as if I didn't tell them," she thought. "They're very rude."

The twins however were enthusiastic and cried encouragingly, "Smashing, Rosie! Never heard anything like it! Keep going!" Then they collapsed in giggles.

She gathered her breath and nerve and Louisa tried to accompany a voice that could not hit one right note:

She set her sister's hair on fire
And as the flames rose higher and higher
She danced around the funeral pyre
Playing her violin – lin – lin – lin
Playing her violin.

She chopped her baby brother in two
And served him up as Irish Stew
And invited the neighbours in – in – in – in –
She invited the neighbours in.

At last a policeman came to call
And she had to confess it all
For she knew to lie was a sin ñsin – sin – sin
Yes!
Forrrrrr –
She knew-hoo to lie-hie was a sih-hih-hih-hih-hinnnnn-nnn-nnn.

As she dragged out the last line Louisa stopped playing and groaned. Mrs Smith wiped her forehead and Amelia rubbed her ears. The middle-aged couple and their son sat stunned.

But the twins clapped loudly and the old man immediately said, "Beautiful. *So* beautiful."

"Sing us another one," Edward cried. His mother jumped up from the piano and said, "No, no, *no!* Time for supper, everyone!"

The twins congratulated Rosie. "You have to teach us that song," Henry said. "And how to sing like that."

Jealous, Amelia said with false sympathy, "It must take years of suffering and pain before you can mangle your voice like that."

Rosie didn't answer. "Cheek!" she thought. "Anyone'd think she didn't sound like a frog."

"Don't mind her," Henry said when Amelia moved away. "We thought your song was smashing. The best we've ever heard." She looked at him for any hint of sarcasm, but he was completely sincere.

Mollie when she arrived with the supper tray had a different reaction. "Did someone take a turn in here?" She whispered to the boys. "We heard a terrible wailing – Cook thought it was a banshee."

"That was Rosie singing," Amelia explained.

"Oh dear, oh dear. The poor, poor girl. Ah well. Sure we all have our cross to bear."

And Mrs Smith murmured rather unkindly, "That is *so* true. I, for one, feel crucified."

Conversation over supper was quiet and soon after the guests made their excuses and left.

Henry told Rosie, "Your singing got rid of that lot.You'll definitely have to show us how to do it. Usually they do another turn after supper."

"And you saved us having to dance," his brother added. "I suppose Mother thought if we followed you we'd only make a show of ourselves. You're the best, Rosie!"

Chapter 13

SUNDAY PASSED quietly. Eleven o'clock mass was followed by lunch. Afterwards Louisa ordered a carriage to take them to the Phoenix Park. "We won't get there on Wednesday," she explained, "so I thought it would be nice to see the rehearsals."

Rosie enjoyed the journey, even if the seats were a little hard and the carriage bounced them up and down along some of the cobbled streets.

Thousands of Dubliners had the same idea. A procession of families made their way to the Fifteen Acres where three thousand foot soldiers and cavalry were practising for the big day. Rosie had never seen so many military. The uniforms were impressive. The infantry marched, the bandsmen played, the cavalry were dashing. An enthusiastic crowd clapped and cheered and waved flags.

After a while they made for the Vice Regal Lodge where, it seemed to Rosie, millions of boys were rehearsing, each group in different uniform. Louisa named some of them: "That's the Royal Hibernian Military School. And over there are the boys from the King's Hospital School. And by the gate you can see The Boys' Brigade and The Church Lads' Brigade."

They stared at the different groups going through their paces. Suddenly Henry said, "It's a pity you couldn't sing your song for the Queen, Rosie."

"That's a great idea!" Edward was enthusiastic. "Could it be arranged, Mother?"

"No, it couldn't!" Their mother was definite.

Next time she saw the doctor, Louisa decided, she would get him to check out the twins' hearing.

Later when she was preparing for bed, Rosie realised she hadn't thought of Donnelly once that day. Yet, when she peered out the window, she wasn't surprised to spot the familiar figure on the street. He had probably followed them all day. And he would keep following them. He would probably be there when they found the gold. What would they do then, she wondered?

It was something they'd best think about.

"We should have some plan for Donnelly," she told the twins next day. "He follows us everywhere. He's not going to let us get away with the gold."

The twins thought about it and eventually Henry said, "There are three of us and only one of him. We should be able to beat him."

"If you're talking about a fight, count me out," Rosie said. "We were lucky in that shed. It was dark and we took him by surprise. And there were five of us. He won't let that happen again."

"We don't have to fight him." Edward mused. "Between us we could fool him. The minute we find the gold, we separate and get him to follow the one he thinks has it. Only they won't have it. One of the other two will. Tactics! That's all we need."

For once the word didn't grate on Rosie's nerves. She

looked at Edward with admiration. "That is very clever," she said. "*Very* clever."

Edward was chuffed."Did I ever tell either of you about the war against Cetshwayo in Zululand? I'm sure you'd find the tactics very interesting –"

"No, we wouldn't!" Rosie and Henry spoke together.

Edward was deflated till Rosie changed the subject, "What about this fourth clue? What do you think it means, Edward?"

All three of them studied the paper:

At the King's harbour find the key beneath the first stand where the iron circles on the right.

"We have to go to Kingstown," Henry said.

"Where Queen Victoria's yacht is coming in," said Rosie. "I read that in the paper. And it was on the tram. But where is it?"

They looked at her in astonishment. "You must know where it is!"

"Well, I don't. Why must I?"

"Because everyone all over Ireland knows it," Henry said. "It's where the ships come in. It's just before Sandycove. Unless it's gone in your day."

Rosie's face cleared, "No, it's not gone. But it's called Dunlaoire, not *King*stown. We don't have kings – or queens – any more."

Their mouths dropped. Then Edward said, "Why not? Did something terrible happen to them?"

"No. England still has them. We don't. We belong to ourselves."

"Ah," Edward said. "You mean you have Home Rule. Pa is always talking about that."

"No, I don't mean that." Rosie wasn't quite sure what Home Rule was, just that Ireland didn't have it. Knowing she wouldn't be able to answer many of their questions, she hurried on, "Look. We're not ruled by England any more. Not most of us, anyway. Right? But it happened ages and ages ago. And there's no time to talk about it now. Not if we're going to solve the last clues!" She waved the piece of paper at him, "What do you think this means? *Find the key beneath the first stand where the iron circles on the right*."

It was Henry who answered, "That's probably the first bandstand. It has iron railings. We'll have to see what the rest means when we get out there."

"And where might that be?" Louisa had just entered the room.

"We're taking Rosie to Kingstown, Mother."

She shook her head. "You can't. Not today. Have you forgotten? You have your piano lessons at midday and this afternoon we have to visit poor old Mrs Lawlor." And she added for Rosie's benefit, "Mrs Lawlor's an elderly neighbour who doesn't get out much anymore."

The boys groaned. "We shouldn't have to do any lessons during the hols," Henry said.

"Of course you should. Your music master insists you need lots of practice."

"And Mrs Lawlor doesn't like us," Henry added.

"Not true. She looks forward to your visits. She especially looks forward to your Irish dancing."

Rosie smiled broadly. It was easier to imagine two horses doing a jig.

The boys were scarlet. "Mother, you know we can't dance," Henry protested. "Mrs Lawlor hates it when we do a reel."

"She does not. She told me you were a wonder."

Louisa could not be persuaded to let them off the visit. "If it's Rosie you're worried about, don't. She will come with us."

In desperation, Edward played a trump card. "Oh good," he said. "She can sing for Mrs Lawlor."

Louisa paled, "No, she can't. Mrs Lawlor has a bad heart. I mean –"

"It's all right," Rosie said. "I don't want to sing. It hurts my throat."

"Not to mention other people's ears, " Louisa muttered.

"Our dancing might make Mrs Lawlor worse." Henry sounded hopeful.

"No, it wouldn't. Last time she said it was incredible what you could do with your feet!"

"Mother! That wasn't a compliment!"

Loisa changed the subject. "You can take Rosie to Kingstown tomorrow," she said. "That will be much more exciting. Her Majesty's arrival will bring out the crowds and Rosie will enjoy all the fanfare."

It was funny, Rosie mused. Louisa had no problem realising Rosie's voice was truly terrible, yet she thought the world of her sons' dancing. Anyone else'd know just to look at them they'd be as good at Irish dancing as Sumo wrestlers would be at ballet.

Not that they looked like Sumo wrestlers, but they weren't exactly graceful.

They weren't much good at the piano either. Rosie stayed in the same room for a while, but soon her nerves jangled and she wandered away to the kitchen at the other end of the house. The piano players could still be heard.

Cook was moaning to herself. She was mixing the ingredients with her hands. When the piano was really bad, she slapped the dough together and threw it about in the bowl.

"Mrs O'Neill should know by now," she told Rosie darkly, "that those boys cannot recognise a single note. They shouldn't be allowed to cause so much agony!"

"I think it's a family failing, " Rosie mused.

Cook rolled up her eyes. "'Tis a family *tragedy!*" she said. "And that's where it should be kept – in the family. Noise like that –" She indicated the piano at the other end of the house, while flinging the dough onto the table –" and singing like yours shouldn't be inflicted on the innocent. There's enough suffering in the world!"

This last observation didn't include the dough, which she punched a number of times and then flattened with the rolling-pin.

Rosie enjoyed the afternoon.

The twins' dancing was desperate. They galloped through a two-hand reel, boots thudding heavily on the floor. Mrs Lawlor sat in her armchair looking sick, as a candlestick was knocked over and ornaments jumped on the mantlepiece.

Rosie had to wipe the tears from her eyes.

"Thank God," she heard Mrs Lawlor groan as the mad clatter came to a halt.

"Pardon?" said Louisa.

"I was just thinking aloud, Mrs O'Neill. Thinking you must often thank God for giving your dear boys this – this –"

"Unique talent?" Louisa supplied.

"Unique? Oh, well. Yes, indeed. Oh, certainly unique." Mrs Lawlor sank back and only perked up when they were leaving.

"God bless your energy," she told the boys. And Rosie, who was last out was the only one who heard her add, "For he certainly didn't bless your dancing!" It was after one when they set off on Tuesday. Already the trams were crowded with those who wanted get a good viewing place for the queen's arrival. For once the roads were full of traffic, all of it making for Kingstown.

The harbour was buzzing with excitement by the time they got there. People were making for the pier as fast as possible. Even grannies were racing, using parasols to jab anyone who got in their way.

"What's happening?" Rosie asked a woman pushing a pram. She found herself running to keep up.

"Her Majesty's yacht! It's four hours early. You can see it beyond the harbour."

Without quite knowing why, Rosie started racing too, the boys right behind her. People were coming from all directions. Once on the pier they were forced to slow down, because of the huge numbers.

"How on earth can we find the key with this crowd?" Rosie wondered.

They were pushed onwards down the pier. While Victoria's yacht wasn't yet visible, they could see frantic activity on the Royal Navy ships docked alongside.

Suddenly there was the sound of gunfire and the crowd shuddered to a halt. It was quickly followed by more volleys.

"The twenty-one-gun salute," Edward explained.

There was a respectful silence then, from the crowds on the pier. Looking down from the sea wall, Rosie saw the Navy bandsmen on each ship, instruments at the ready. Crews stood to attention on every deck and at some mysterious signal the bands played *God Save The Queen*. As the voices of the sailors rose in unison, people on the pier began to join in, till almost everyone was singing in welcome.

A man stopped and gave Rosie a dig, "Sing up, child."

"I don't know it, " she said politely. The man stared at her, turned away and sang twice as loudly as before.

When it was finished, word went round that Her Majesty's boat was staying out in the bay. Soon the crowd was on the move again, this time more orderly, but still anxious to catch a glimpse of royalty.

At the end of the pier, looking across to Howth, Rosie saw the *Victoria and Albert* with its escort of four grey warships.

"Tonight all the ships will be illuminated with coloured lights," Henry told her.

"Maybe they'll look a bit more interesting than they do now," Rosie said.

A woman turned to glare at her and Henry went, "Sshhh."

Then she saw that all the smaller boats in the harbour had upped anchor and set out to sea, honking, sending up streamers of welcome. Soon the flotilla was circling the ships in the bay. People on the harbour walls clapped and shouted.

Rosie could not feel a part of it.

"This would be a good time to look at that bandstand," Henry said.

"What about the crowds?" Rosie said.

"They're only interested in Her Majesty's yacht. No one will be looking at us."

They made their way against the flow back to the first bandstand. To escape the pushing they climbed onto the wooden platform. It was perched on four sets of blocks to stop it rotting underneath.

The stand was empty and they could study the railings that went the whole way round on either side of the steps. A design of wrought-iron circles filled each gap between the upright rails.

"Which of those two is the first one?" Edward pointed at the circles on either side of the entrance.

"We'll have to go under and see," Rosie said.

No one paid any attention to the three youngsters as they slithered beneath the stand. The smell was musty and when their eyes adjusted to the shadows, they saw rubbish – paper bags, broken bottles, tins. There was a scurrying sound that Rosie hoped wasn't rats. A lot of muck had piled up behind the blocks. Rosie cleared some of it with the toe of her boot and the twins scraped at the rest with penknives.

Their fingers edged around each block under the iron circles, but they could feel nothing except slime and nuggets of dust that separated into powder at a touch.

"Where is this stupid key?" Rosie said.

"We'll have to dig." Edward started scraping at the soil with his knife, not making much headway.

"Oh great. We should get to Australia in no time." Rosie was sarcastic.

"The clay is easier over here," Henry was digging away on the other side of the entrance.

Rosie looked at the tiny hole he'd made. "That'll be a really good tunnel any minute," she told him.

He ignored her, digging madly. "There's something here!" Flinging down the knife he attacked the soil with his hands. The other two joined him now, scrabbling away till they felt a different surface.

"It's a small box, " Rosie said, her voice rising in excitement.

Tracing the edges with their fingers they dug deep and soon Henry pulled out a very old, very dirty tin box. He shook it and they listened in triumph to the rattle. Rust and age had jammed the lid and Edward had to prise it open with his knife.

Inside was the key. Each of them took turns to hold it.

"One more clue!" Rosie swallowed. The boys nodded, unable to speak.

Edward put the key in his pocket and they slid back out into the sunlight.

Chapter 14

ON THEIR way up the pier Rosie was surprised at how many funny looks she got from people in the crowd.

"Is there something wrong with me?" She turned to the twins and immediately saw what was up. They were filthy. At every step a layer of dust shook off them. Their boots and clothes were covered in muck. In fact only their eyelids were clean. These looked very odd, like little white crescent moons against their muddy faces.

Then Edward smiled, teeth startling in his filthy face. "Rosie, you'd think you rolled around in a bog!"

"The same for you and Henry."

In dismay they studied themselves. Rosie's once white, crisp over-dress (which Mollie now washed each night and dried by the range) was streaked and caked. She rubbed at the dirt and saw that her hands were black.

A middle-aged woman stopped. "You are a disgrace!" she told them. "How dare you come in this state to see your gracious Queen. It is an insult!" She marched on, nose in the air.

"It's not deliberate," Rosie called after her. "And she's not my Queen!"

A few people turned around and the boys hustled her away, faces boiling.

At the top of the pier about twenty people gathered in front of a man who was standing on a wooden box.

"No Irish person should be here today! No Irish person should be paying homage to this queen." His shouting drew a bigger group, Rosie and the twins among them.

He was a man in his thirties, tallish. He looked at the crowd over a single eyeglass, his face grave. The more Rosie studied him, the more familiar he seemed. She could not place him. She stared at the hair that flopped into his eyes, the dark suit and the flowing cravat.

"It is a disgrace," he went on, "that you have come to welcome an English queen!"

Some in the crowd began to boo.

"A national disgrace!" he repeated.

It was the voice that placed him suddenly for Rosie. He was that poet, what's his name? Mr Yeats. And he'd been very nice to her in 1920. He was a lot younger this time. No wonder she hadn't recognised him.

"Queen Victoria is the head of an unjust empire, an unjust government!"

There were more catcalls this time and one or two in the crowd shook a fist at the speaker.

A man in front of Rosie waved what looked like a whiskey bottle. "Ah now, lads. Can't we all be friends. Sure isn't it a lovely day?"

Mr Yeats raised his voice again, "Unjust!" He shouted. "Unjust to Ireland! Unjust to the Republic of South Africa! The Boers –"

"Boers! You're the biggest bore of all!" Someone yelled and the crowd laughed.

"And you, sir, are a disgrace!" Yeats's eyeglass glinted with indignation.

"Ah Mister, would you not be upsettin' yourself," The man with the whiskey bottle was in fine form, swaying back and forwards. "Isn't it a great day for Ireland all the same?"

Those around him cheered. Rosie felt sorry for Mr Yeats, but the poet was unshaken.

"It is *not* a great day for Ireland! "he was roaring. "You should not be here. I would ask you to boycott the Queen's visit and to come instead tomorrow night to the meeting of the people –"

"Sure what's wrong with you, man?" The whiskey man was very jolly. " Aren't we all entitled to a holiday? And isn't Her Majesty entitled to a holiday, after sixty years on the throne? Hasn't she served us well? There she's been, lookin' after us all as girl and woman, queen and empress, mother and grandmother. Why wouldn't we welcome her? "

By now everyone was cheering the fellow and a few hefty men lifted him onto their shoulders, where he had a fit of the hiccups and took a swig from the bottle. But those nearer to Mr Yeats were more aggressive. As Rosie moved forward she could see their angry faces and their raised fists.

"Anyways," the whiskey drinker shouted and the crowd went quiet again, "anyways, as I was sayin'. Let's enjoy ourselves. An' let's give Her Majesty a hooley she'll remember for as long as she lives."

People went wild, cheering. Those carrying the man waved their arms and jumped up and down with enthusiasm, forgetting their cargo who fell into the crowd and disappeared for a minute.

From the corner of her eye Rosie could see a group of policemen on the fringes, beginning to move towards the poet, who was looking very disappointed. She wanted to warn him, but he was focusing on the drunken fellow who had righted himself and was now roaring out again, "Have a good time, man! don't be so miserable. Sure won't it be *all* the same in a hundred years' time!"

This made the poet look so depressed that Rosie felt obliged to shout, "No, it won't! It won't be at all the same in a hundred years' time. There'll be no English king or queen over us then!"

The boys groaned. The poet looked down and smiled at her, welcoming support even from a filthy ragamuffin.

People around her were raging. Someone jabbed her with a brolly and hissed, "How dare you!"

One policeman had heard her and struggled in her direction. The group holding the whiskey-drinker started singing, "God Save the Queen." Those near Mr Yeats booed and shouted. They surged forward, intent on throwing the poet off his box. At the same time the police muscled their way through, a half dozen or so, head and shoulders over the crowd, spiked helmets catching the sunlight.

Rosie tried to disappear, but found herself gripped and pulled by a huge hand. She had no choice but to follow. At the same time Mr Yeats was seized and bundled through a crowd that wanted to bash him up. One fellow even took a swing at him, but hit someone else who promptly whacked him back. Soon there was a free-for-all, as Rosie and the poet were dragged free and bundled into a police wagon where they sat on a bench. It was very much like a van, only horse-drawn.

"I wish you wouldn't do this, Mr Yeats!" a red-faced policeman told him, as his companions went back to stop the fight. "You could have been badly injured. And lord knows we have enough to do this week, what with all the drinking and celebrating, without poets adding to the upset!"

Mr Yeats adjusted his cravat and gazed at the roof of the van. "What are poets for," he murmured, "if not to cause upset?"

But the policeman had turned his attention to Rosie, "As for you! You're every bit as bad as him. Worse! At least Mr

Yeats is a gentleman and properly turned out. Not a ragamuffin! A ragamuffin who disturbs the peace and commits treason and doesn't know what she's talking about."

Rosie was furious and opened her mouth to say so, but the policeman wasn't finished, not by a long shot. "You should be locked up," he went on. "Imagine turning up all filthy to see Her Majesty. What kind of respect is that for a dear old lady? And then telling everyone she won't be here in a hundred years' time. Well, she won't, but she wouldn't want to be reminded of that, would she? It's not polite, so it's not."

Rosie managed to protest, "I didn't say that. And anyway she couldn't hear me. She's out on her ship. And I am not a filthy ragamuffin –"

"You are so. Why, you look as if you've been rolling in a rubbish dump for a week. And as for Her Majesty not knowing what you've said – well you can take it from me, the dear lady doesn't have to be standing beside you to hear those unkind words. Oh no!"

He rocked back and forth on his heels, nodding his head very seriously.

Amazed, Rosie said, "Has she got magnificent hearing then?"

Now she was sorry she hadn't read her History books. They must surely mention that Queen Victoria could hear what someone said from more than a mile away. It was probably in the *Guinness Book of Records* too.

Mr Yeats sniggered and the policeman grew redder. "Don't you be so cheeky, girl. Of course she can't hear you, as such, out in the bay. But someone could tell her how unkind one of her subjects is. Then where would we be?"

"But I'm not one of her subjects!" Rosie cried.

"Hear hear!" said the poet and smiled at her.

"I'll not listen to this." the policeman started shouting. "You should both be arrested."

Mr Yeats gazed at the spike on his helmet, "But, my dear man, we *are* arrested."

For an answer, the policeman slammed the van door. They heard him climb up onto the front seat and flick the reins. The horsed began to trot and the passengers in the back almost fell off the bench as the van bounced up and down.

"Well, I must say you're a brave young lady," Mr Yeats said. "Even if you are a mite filthy."

Rosie didn't feel at all brave. "Are they going to put us in prison?" she asked.

"Not at all. They're just rescuing us. We'll be let out with a caution in a little while." He leaned towards her. "They did us a favour you know. That crowd was very unfriendly." He seemed hurt.

"They probably didn't recognise you," Rosie comforted him. "They don't realise you're a famous poet. That's 'cos poets aren't as easy to recognise as pop stars and movie stars."

Mr Yeats was astonished. He knew nothing of pop stars or movie stars, but found it incredible that this filthy child, who looked a bit like a tramp, knew of him.

"I don't suppose you know any of my poems?" It was too much to expect, he thought.

"Well, I learned to sing 'Down by The Salley Gardens'," Rosie told him. She frowned, remembering the choir teacher's expression of agony.

"To *sing* it? My goodness. You actually learned to *sing* it?" The poet, who didn't yet know his poem had become a famous song, was chuffed. "Oh, please," he said. "Will you sing it for me?"

Rosie's heart sank. She knew poets were sensitive. She knew the effect of her voice. She didn't want to be rude, but she didn't want a poet to have a nervous breakdown on her account.

"I'm sorry," she told him, "I can't sing."

His face fell, "But you must. You said you learned to sing it. Please, don't be shy."

Oh God. Rosie felt stricken. But she knew it was nothing to how he'd feel if she sang.

"No, I can't." She swallowed, aware of his disappointment. Her face reddened and she tried to explain. "I was expelled from the school choir. That's 'cos my voice is terrible. The teacher said I destroyed every song. So if I sing your poem, I'll destroy it too."

Desperately wanting to change the subject, Rosie suddenly remembered, "Oh we learned another poem by you as well – 'Red Hanrahan's Song about Ireland' –"

She stopped, aware she had committed some terrible blunder.

His face had paled and he was swallowing rapidly. As yet the poem she mentioned was little more than a few rough verses. It wasn't finished. It hadn't been published, hadn't even been shown to anyone else.

"Er . . . I've forgotten how that poem starts. Could you remind me, please?" His voice was low, almost shaking.

"Okay." Rosie was relieved to think he was upset because he'd forgotten some of his poem.

> *The old brown thorn-trees break in two high over Cummen Strand*
> *Under a bitter black wind that blows from the left hand. . .*

"That's the first two lines," she said. "Do you want any more?"

He was staring at her and she had to repeat the question.

"What? Oh no. That's fine. Thank you."

What an extraordinary child, he thought. She didn't look as if she went to school, never mind learned poetry and singing, though now that he studied her, he could see that her clothes were quite good, if a bit large for her. And then there was her certainty. Saying there'd be no king or queen of Ireland in a hundred years' time. She spoke differently too. Using words he didn't know, when he knew most words. What had she said? Pop stars and movie stars. And strangest of all, she knew "Red Hanrahan".

Eyes narrowed, he studied her.

Rosie shifted uncomfortably and wondered if he was still insulted that she wouldn't sing.

But then he smiled, and his words took her breath away. "Do you come from a different time?"

It was her turn to lose colour. He went on, "I ask because I am very interested in such things. There is wisdom to be learned by contact with people from other times, who have lived other lives. I've tried to reach them with seances, though with little success. I've tried so hard. How strange if fate has arranged this meeting without any effort on my part. Tell me. Please. It would mean so much. Are you from another time?"

She had barely nodded her head when the police van jolted to a stop. Rosie fell onto the floor and by the time she'd gathered her wits, the door was open and the policeman was sternly telling them they were free.

"But, mind you!" he said to Rosie, "There'll be no more public disorder, d'you hear!"

She nodded and before he could give out further, she'd jumped out of the van and rushed away.

"Stop, girl. Stop!" Mr Yeats jumped out after her, but already she was disappearing round a corner.

He sighed. Had she nodded that time when he'd asked her, or had he imagined it? Was she from another time? If so, it definitely wasn't the past. He concentrated and her words on the pier came rushing back: *No, it won't be all the same in a hundred years' time. There'll be no English king or queen over us then*. A message from the future.

Suddenly he felt very happy. Lost in thought he went on his way, not hearing the policeman's warnings.

The policeman sighed, "Probably making up one of his poems," he thought. "And that's what he should stick to, instead of trying to change what can't be changed."

They had been dropped off at Merrion, so within fifteen minutes Rosie was back at the house. She reckoned the boys would have started for home as soon as she'd been arrested, but wouldn't yet have arrived. They'd be busy thinking of a way to tell Louisa what had happened. There was no sign of Donnelly, so she waited outside, smiling to herself as she imagined their relief at seeing her.

"You do look revolting!"

There was only one person who drawled like that.

"Do I, Amelia?"

If Amelia had been more observant she'd have seen a dangerous glint in the other girl's eye. Rosie was fed up being told how awful she looked.

"Yes, you do. Really filthy. Mother says girls who get dirty are rough and common."

"Is that so?" Rosie's voice was even but her temper was beginning to boil.

The other smirked, "It's a good idea to wash sometimes. You should bathe at least once a week. Hasn't anyone ever told you that?"

Glaring at her, Rosie said, "When I'm at home I have a shower every day!"

"A shower!" Amelia's tinkling laugh got on Rosie's nerves. "I suppose that means you stand out in a drizzle and hope to get rid of some of the filth." She reached over, flicked some dirt from Rosie's jacket and gave a genteel shudder.

Rosie snapped, "Don't you touch me!" She pushed her

away, opened the gate and went into the garden, intent on getting away from Amelia's insults. But Amelia followed her.

"Ugh. Look at the streaks on my dress! How dare you! You're a dirty tramp." Amelia shoved Rosie, who shoved back. Shrieking with rage and disgust, Amelia kicked out. Rosie dodged and the other girl fell into the flowerbeds. Rosie could not resist kicking a bit of extra clay onto her blue dress.

Hysterical now, Amelia began tearing up flowers and plants and flinging them at Rosie, along with muck and pebbles, all the time bawling insults. "Filthy slut! Hussy! Dirty cow!"

Carried away, she did not see what Rosie saw.

The door had opened. Cook, Mollie and Louisa stood in the entrance, mesmerised for some moments, as Amelia destroyed the flowerbed and attacked Rosie.

Then Louisa rushed down, right in the firing line. A hail of clay, stones and petals hit her arm. Outraged, Louisa pulled Amelia up. "What do you think you're doing?"

Amelia started blubbering with shock, but there was no stopping Louisa. "Just wait till your mother hears about this. You are *very* nasty. And I wouldn't have believed it if I hadn't seen you myself! Just look at the garden! Look at the path! Look at my clothes! Such dreadful behaviour! A common ruffian would have more manners."

She had to pause for breath, since she was pushing Amelia down the garden path as well as giving out. Amelia didn't want to go. She wanted to explain.

"It was her fault –" she bawled.

Louisa shook her. "You forget," she said coldly. "I saw what happened. Rosie was just standing there while you – you –" Her voice shook "You pelted her with muck. Look at the poor child. One would think she'd been in a rubbish dump. And you ruined our garden!"

Amelia opened her mouth once more, but Louisa had

pushed her out the gate and closed it. "Off with you! At once! No more lies, please! I shall see your mother later." She swung around, put a sympathetic arm around Rosie and led her inside.

Amelia bawled her way home.

Inside, Rosie was treated like a war-victim. Mollie filled a hot tub and took away her clothes for washing. Louisa found her a clean shift and dressing-gown and blamed every speck of dirt on the horrible Amelia. After her bath Cook gave her home-made lemonade and ginger cake with fudge-lemon icing.

"This is the most beautiful cake I've ever tasted," she told Cook earnestly.

"Well, you'd need to build your strength up after such a horrible attack!" Cook was still indignant on her behalf. "That Amelia one is far too sneaky. Oh, butter wouldn't melt in her mouth with a grown-up. But look at the state she left you in! Filthy. Absolutely filthy."

Sometimes life worked out well, Rosie thought. She sighed with contentment, surrounded by gentle adults and stuffing her face in the warm kitchen.

Which was how the twins found her when they came home tired out, having waited for more than an hour in the long queues for a tram, all the time worrying about Rosie, thinking she was in a police cell and wondering how on earth they were going to tell their mother.

Their relief at seeing her scoffing food in the kitchen was mixed with envy. She looked so comfortable. And clean. Rosie smiled at them, her mouth too full to talk. Three pairs of adult eyes studied their appearance.

"Please explain," Louisa said, her voice dangerously calm, "what happened to the immaculate clothes you went out in this morning?"

They looked at Rosie, wondering what explanation she'd

given. Whatever it had been, it had worked wonders. She looked back at them, unable to help.

"Well? Henry? Edward? I'm waiting. What were you up to?"

Reluctantly Edward said, "We were under a bandstand on Kingstown pier. It was very mucky."

"Under a – under a bandstand? You were playing under a bandstand?" Louisa felt bewildered, then angry. "Why on earth would any sane person go under a bandstand? You must have had to crawl. No wonder you look like coalmen. And now I suppose you expect poor Mollie to wash your clothes?" She paused, and a fresh reason for annoyance occured to her. "And why did you not stay with your cousin? Then she mightn't have suffered so badly. You were responsible for your cousin. Why didn't you look after her?"

Rosie and the twins stared at each other, the boys trying in vain to work out why she was getting royal treatment while they were in disgrace.

At last Rosie murmured, "I got a lift before them."

"That's right, Mother." Edward said eagerly. "Rosie got earlier transport. There were such crowds waiting on the trams!"

Louisa still looked at them coldly. "That may be an excuse for getting separated but not for the state of your clothes. You will take a bath and then, as punishment, you will mow the lawn and repair the damage done to the front garden. And you will go without tea."

The boys looked sadly at Cook and Molly, but found no sympathy. Molly was thinking of the time it would take to wash their clothes and Cook could see that the kitchen floor would need to be scrubbed after their great dirty boots. Only Rosie was happy, still munching away.

She'd been as filthy as them, the twins thought. And worse than them, she'd disturbed the peace and been arrested for helping to start a riot. Yet here she was being rewarded! It wasn't fair. Sometimes life worked out very badly.

Chapter 15

"WE HAVE to find the treasure tonight," Rosie whispered to the twins.

It was after dinner and they were around the table in the small sitting-room. Louisa was reading by the fire.

"That's very easy to say," Edward replied. "But where is the treasure? There's no point sneaking out unless we know where we're going."

"It's obvious where it is, " Rosie said. "It's in the fifth clue." She took out the paper. "It's where furniture is made, beneath the pale boards."

"Very helpful," Edward muttered sarcastically. "Very clear!"

"Let's put together the answers we have, "Henry suggested. "Then we can try and make some sense of them. Let's write them out."

He fetched an inkwell and a pen. Rosie took out her clues and Henry dipped the nib in the ink and began to write beside each one:

1. Arthur Jones.
2. French.
3. Chest.
4. The key.
5. ?

He turned to Rosie. "What does that fifth clue mean? *Where furniture is made beneath pale boards*."

"It must be a furniture factory," she said. "Don't you have any names of places where furniture is made?"

"Arthur Jones," said Louisa, looking up a moment from her book.

They swivelled around to stare at her, but she was lost again in her story.

"Excuse me, Louisa," Rosie said. "What do you mean, 'Arthur Jones'?"

She looked up again. "You mentioned something about furniture," she said vaguely.

"Yes. Yes we did!" They tried to hurry her along.

"Well, it's just that 'Arthur Jones' has the best furniture shop and workrooms in Dublin." Her eyes went back to her book.

They took a deep breath. Rosie looked at the twins accusingly. "How is it you don't know this?"

"Why would we know about furniture shops?" Edward was amazed.

"Anyway, we know now." Henry said. He turned to his mother. "Is 'Arthur Jones' a shop in town?"

She frowned. "Really, Henry. Stop interrupting my reading. I'm just at the exciting part. Arthur Jones is in Stephen's Green, though why you have this sudden interest in furniture is beyond me." Suddenly she focused her attention as if he might be up to something.

"It's just a puzzle we're doing, Mother."

"Mmm. Well, furniture is made in the workrooms and a lot is imported from France. The place has been there for years. Now *please*. Let me concentrate." Once more she returned to her story.

Agog, they looked at each other.

Then slowly Henry put the clues together so that at last they made sense. "We'll find the sovereigns in 'Arthur Jones' furniture shop, in the workroom, in a French chest which this key opens. Is that right?"

They nodded and Rosie added. "The French chest might be underneath the floor in the workroom. See where it says, *Beneath the pale boards*."

"We've solved all the clues," Edward said slowly.

"And we've got to find the gold tonight, "Rosie said. "Before Joseph comes home and calls the police."

"But Donnelly might have given up," Henry said. "I didn't see him at all today, did you?"

"No, but I bet he was there." Rosie was certain. "He won't give up after thirty years in jail. I bet if you look out the window, he'll be near the street lamp. He was there last night and the night before."

As the boys took this in, she continued, "When Joseph finds he's still around he'll get the police. And if they catch Donnelly he'll tell them we have the clues rather than let us get the gold."

"He's sure to follow us if we go out tonight." Edward shivered at the prospect, but Henry said,"Rosie's right. We've got to go. Anyway he won't be expecting us to be out late. If we leave by the back lane, we might give him the slip."

"That's a brilliant idea!"

Now the ideas came fast.

"We'll go to bed early, pretend to be tired."

"Then we'll sneak out."

"Get a late tram."

"We'll have to break into Arthur Jones."

"There'll be a trade entrance round the back. All shops have them."

"Maybe we can force a window."

"I'll bring my torch. It'll give us some light."

She had to explain what it was and how it worked and they were almost as interested in the torch as in the gold.

"Imagine, we could have a huge fortune in our hands tonight," Rosie got them back on track.

With growing excitement they thought of the night ahead.

Then Henry said, "Let's go to bed now, then sneak out at nine o'clock. I heard Mother ask Cook for an early supper then. We can go through the kitchen when she's serving supper."

"I thought that was Molly's job," Rosie said.

"It is. But she has an evening off."

Louisa looked startled when they said goodnight.

"Don't you want to see Pa?" Then she answered her own question. "I suppose you're worried as to what he'll have to say about today. But I won't tell him. So you may wait up if you like."

Henry began to yawn massively and after a second the other two followed his example. They were so convincing Louisa had to stifle her own yawns.

"Perhaps you're wise," she told them. "After all, we have an exciting day ahead of us tomorrow."

Not half as exciting as tonight, Rosie thought as they made their way upstairs.

It was a chilly evening and Rosie did not know whether she was shivering from the cold or from fear and anticipation. She reckoned it would be worse outside. In any case, to get a bit warmer she put on a pair of the navy bloomers Louisa had given her. They tied with a pink ribbon just below the knee, over her long socks.

"Yuck!" She was disgusted at her reflection in the mirror. With her heavy boots, the long socks and the really horrible baggy knickers, she was not beautiful. And Rosie thought, "Oh God, that is *sick!*" A good thing nobody in her class could see her. But at least she was warmer.

At nine o'clock they waited on the lower landing till they heard Cook go into the small sitting-room. Then they sped swiftly and as silently as possible down the stairs, along the hall, through the kitchen and out the back door.

Rosie followed the boys down the garden path. They stopped at a tallish gate leading onto a lane. Rusted with disuse, the gate screeched when they tried to open it.

"We'll have to climb over. Otherwise we'll be heard,' Edward whispered.

The boys managed, no problem, but climbing over an iron gate in a long skirt was not something Rosie was used to. In jeans she was agile. In this gear she was clumsy and slow.

"Girls!" Henry muttered. "They're useless at climbing."

"You try doing it in these clothes!" Rosie snapped. She was astride the top when the gate chose to swing slowly open, screeching like a cat in agony.

"Hurry, Rosie. Mother will be out." The boys pulled her off the gate and she fell on top of them, but within a minute they were racing down the lane and onto the street.

Donnelly had heard the noise cut through the dark silence. He sped round the corner, keeping close to the hedges and was in time to see them turning down a side road.

"They're in a right hurry and they wouldn't be out at night unless it was important," he reasoned.

He kept out of sight, but they hardly looked back, almost certain the noise of the gate wouldn't have travelled so far.

They did check at the tram stop, but were satisfied no one else was around. It was only when they'd gone upstairs and the tram was moving that Donnelly rushed from his hiding-place, caught up and jumped on.

At Stephen's Green they didn't even look around. If they had done they might have spotted the lurking figure, for the moon had risen and the night was cold and clear.

But they were sure he was keeping watch at his usual look-out.

'Arthur Jones' was a large impressive shop, its window display lit up inside by the new- fangled electric lighting.

"How could you not know about this place?" Rosie said. "It's huge."

Edward explained, "We don't pay much attention to furniture. It's not very interesting, is it?" Noticing her scornful look, he added, "I suppose you know Grafton Street really well? In your day, I mean."

"Yes, I do. So?"

"So is there a furniture shop there?"

She frowned, "I don't really know. You're right. A furniture shop isn't noticeable."

They made their way down a narrow street to the lane at the back of the shop. The place was deserted and there were no lights here. A small wooden cart rested against the heavy locked door. The large window was at least six foot from the ground.

"We can use the cart to get onto the ledge."

It seemed so simple. They trundled the cart over. But when Henry climbed onto the side, it see-sawed and he fell off.

Rosie and Edward held it level while he climbed on again, but the window-ledge was way beyond his reach.

"Edward, you'll have to get up here, so I can climb on your shoulders."

Edward clambered on willingly, but Rosie could not hold the cart steady as one hunkered down, trying to keep his balance, and the other climbed up his back. The handles jerked out of her grip and both boys tumbled into the lane.

"Right. It'll have to be you, Rosie," said Henry. "You're the lightest. Edward will hold the cart. I'll balance on the side and you climb onto my shoulders. Can you do it?"

His remark about girls still rankled and Rosie said, "Of course I can do it, but only if I'm dressed more like you."

Before they could say anything, she gathered her skirt up and began tucking it into her long knickers.

Oh God. At first the boys didn't know where to look. They were not used to bloomers. Then they started to snort. "Rosie, you look like a huge onion with arms and legs!"

Soon they were in convulsions.

Rosie waited patiently while they slapped each other on the back and roared laughing. When they'd finally wiped their eyes she said, "Finished?" They nodded. "Are you sure? 'Cos Henry, I don't want you having another fit when I'm on your shoulders. Right?"

"Right. Sorry, Rosie."

This time the plan worked. Edward held the cart. Rosie climbed onto Henry's shoulders and when he carefully managed to stand, she wobbled into an upright positition. Without giving herself time to think, she heaved herself up until she was kneeling on the ledge.

"Humpty Dumpty," Edward murmured and Henry took a fit of laughing.

Ignoring them and gripping the sash, she stood upright. By the light of the moon, she could see into what looked like a storeroom. She tugged at the window. It didn't budge and she could see a small metal bar holding it in place.

"Give me your penknife, Henry."

The boy opened the knife and stretched up, handle towards her. Rosie had to kneel to reach it. Then she inserted the blade under the sash and pushed, hoping the bar wasn't stiff with paint or lack of use.After a second it moved aside. Rosie stood, dropped the knife to Henry, lifted the window and climbed through.

Groping her way through the storeroom, she made her way around to the door, pulled back the bolt and opened it.

"You're smashing, Rosie," Edward told her.

"Even though you look like a massive balloon," added Henry.

Taking the torch from her jacket pocket, Rosie lit their way through the building. Behind the shop itself were storerooms, offices and, at last, the workroom they were looking for. Standing in the doorway they shone the torch around the benches, the machinery and the unfinished pieces of furniture. The room was at the side of the building and the moonlight streamed in through two large windows, making the torch almost unnecessary.

Even from the doorway they could see where the floorboards under the glass had been whitened by years of sun.

Edging their way carefully through the cluttered room, they were soon studying the wood for signs of a hiding-place.

"Perhaps there's a knob you push," Rosie said, remembering the secret panel in Oak Park. They pressed every square inch of the whitened wood, but nothing gave way.

"Maybe there's a switch on the wall behind," suggested Edward.

Again they pressed each section of the wall, hoping for a board to spring up. Nothing happened.

They groaned, leaning against the wall and staring at the floor, trying to think.

Then Henry said, "There's a wider gap between those two boards than there is between any of the others." They followed the direction of his pointed finger. The gap was about half an inch wide.

"And the plank is shorter and wider than any of the others," Rosie said. It was true. The rest of the boards were around ten feet long and six inches wide – this one measured roughly two square feet.

Immediately Edward went to one of the work benches and took a chisel. Then swiftly he knelt. The edge of the chisel fitted easily into the gap and he levered gently. The board was stiff, but he worked at it and it came up easily enough.

Now all three were on the floor, eagerly lifting the plank to one side. Rosie shone her torch into the darkness. "There's something there," she said. "A kind of hump shape."

Edward drew his fingers over the object. "It's covered in dust." He pushed and the hump moved slightly. They hardly dared believe their search was over.

It was Henry who finally said what they were thinking. "It's the treasure-chest. It has to be."

He leaned in and hauled it out. So much dust was dislodged that it set them coughing and wheezing. Tears streamed and they had to step back to recover breath.

When the air had settled, Rosie lifted it onto a table, found an old oily rag beside a machine and vigorously wiped the box clean, paying particular attention to the keyhole in front. Henry found a polishing cloth and soon the chest had lost its neglected look.

"It's beautiful," Rosie said. And so it was, with its curved lid and light mahogany wood. Two bands of gold stretched over the top and down the front, on either side of the golden keyhole. Two figures were carved on the lid, a young man presenting a lady with a miniature version of the box.

"It's very old," Edward said.

"I think it might have been a jewellry box," Rosie mused.

Henry took the key from his trousers pocket. It turned in the lock effortlessly, a sign of the superb craft that had fashioned the box. They closed their eyes as he lifted the lid and when they looked they were almost dazzled by the gold coins gleaming and winking in the moonlight.

They breathed deep and sighed, their quest over. Suddenly Rosie dipped her hand into the chest and lifted a fistful of coins, letting them rain down again. The other two did the same and the sovereigns cascaded in a small golden waterfall through their fingers.

"We did it!" Rosie breathed. "We solved those clues and we found the treasure."

"Yahoo!" Edward gave a shout of joy. Henry linked Rosie's arm on one side and Edward's on the other and all three did a gallop around the tables and the benches and the unfinished furniture.

"Yahoo!" Edward shouted.

"Yahoo!" the others echoed.

"We did it! We did it! We did it!" they shouted, galloping back to the chest.

Edward was the first to calm down. He lifted the chest. "We'd best go," he said. "We can decide tomorrow what to do with this."

"When we get near home, we'd better watch out for Donnelly."

Two things happened very quickly then.

First the night-watchman, who'd been having a snooze in his own little hide-away, was rudely awakened by the commotion. Still dopy, he wondered for a few mad moments were there wild animals in the workroom. Then he heard the young voices.

"*Chiselurs!*" he spluttered. "Having a hooley! I'll get them!" And he rushed into the workroom, waving a sturdy stick.

No sooner had the three gasped with dismay at this, than someone stepped through the doorway and hit the watchman on the back of the head with a metal object. He crumpled to the floor, out cold.

Behind him stood Donnelly, his huge shape distorted by the moon. He was blocking their exit, pointing something at them.

Terror gripped them as they realised he was holding a gun.

Chapter 16

DONNELLY WAVED the gun at Edward and indicated the box. "Hand that over," he snarled.

Edward was slow to move and Rosie said sharply, "Do as he says. He could kill you."

Donnelly sneered, "If you're not inclined to take her advice, lad, just look at this fellow." He nudged the watchman with his foot. Edward gave him the chest and he gripped it under his left arm.

"My my, don't you look nice?" he said to Rosie. "Just like a giant marrow. Going to a fancy-dress party after this, were you?"

When she didn't answer, he snarled,"Well, there'll be no more parties for you lot. I'm going to lock you into a nice secure place, that you won't ever get out of."

He motioned them out of the workroom and along a corridor. "Stop there and open that door!"

Henry obeyed his order and he pushed them into a room that was not much larger than a cupboard. There were no windows and it was pitch black. As they stumbled in the darkness, Donnelly slammed the door shut and bolted it on the outside.

Edward threw himself against it. "You let us out!" He

shouted. "We'll get the police after you!" Donnelly laughed and they heard his footsteps echo down the corridor.

"We'll be stuck here all night," Edward said.

"And it was all for nothing," sighed Henry.

"And tomorrow we'll be in terrible trouble!" Rosie groaned.

"And you're taking up all the room in here, Rosie, with your dress like that." Henry told her.

Swiftly she untucked it.

"Sssh. Listen!" Edward said.

They heard the footsteps returning.

"This should keep you nice and warm," Donnelly grunted. He was stuffing paper along the bottom of the door. Then they heard the trickle of liquid and the sound of a can as it dropped on the floor.

"I'd like to shoot you," Donnelly said, "but there's more chance of this looking like an accident. See, the door will burn down and then nobody'll realise it was bolted on the outside." He laughed. "The police will think you broke in to rob the place and you started a fire to cover your tracks. Only you got trapped. Clever, don't you think?"

He laughed again and they heard the sudden spurt of flame and the crackle of fire.

"May you rot in hell!" Donnelly called. He laughed, "And I'll drink to that in The Ivy this very night."

Then he was gone.

Now they could hear the flames gathering energy and they launched themselves against the door which would not budge. Soon the smoke crept in and they began to cough. The air was stifling and they tried to hold their breath but the back of their throats itched like mad and their eyes streamed.

"Get back! Get away from the door!" someone outside roared at them. They moved into the wall, spluttering, and suddenly the door was rammed in and fell. The watchman threw down the plank of wood, rushed in over the blazing door and seized Rosie. "Out!" he shouted. "All of you. Run like hell!"

They stumbled out and he pushed them up the corridor. The fire began to blaze after them, through the warren of rooms where he led them, into the shop.

"No time to get the keys," he muttered. Seizing a small chest of drawers he flung it at the window and the glass shattered. He smashed the jagged edges with a plant-table and they clambered out to the safety of the pavement.

"That villain tried to kill us!" The watchman was fuming. "He tried to burn us alive. If I hadn't recovered we'd be still in there, like burnt rashers."

"You were very brave," Rosie said.

"You saved our lives," the twins told him.

But he wasn't listening, furious at the idea that someone had tried to murder him.

"Well, I caught a good look at the blackguard when he was running away like the coward he is!" he fumed. "And I'll give the police his description, don't you worry!"

At this point a crowd was gathering as the building went up like a matchstick. And a couple told him, "We saw a fellow rushing from the building. We saw him clearly!"

"So much wood in there. It might as well be a bonfire," groaned the watchman.

There was a sound of galloping and a wailing noise. The horse-drawn Fire Brigade and police vans came rushing from Chatham Street and Winetavern Street.

"We can't get caught by the police," Henry whispered to the others. "We could be charged with breaking into the place."

As the watchman ran over to tell the police what had happened, the three melted away from the scene.

"What do we do now?" Rosie was glum.

"If we just go home we're letting Donnelly get away with everything," Edward said.

"We're so late now, we might as well stay out longer," Henry reasoned. "We'll get into the same trouble at home."

"Right then." Rosie summed up their wishes. "Let's find 'The Ivy'. Then we'll find Donnelly." She shivered. "He'll be drinking to our deaths."

Henry said, "Good. That means he won't be expecting us to turn up alive. Maybe we can take him by surprise and get the coins back."

It took them some time to find 'The Ivy'. And they had to put up with a lot when they asked people where it was.

"The Ivy?" said one man. "Pub, is it? Thirsty, are you? Dying for a pint?" And he laughed at his hilarious joke, then added, "Sorry. Never heard of it." And he went off delighted with himself..

Next they tried a woman, not realising till it was too late that she must've come out of a pub herself. She was wearing a shawl and was clutching a jug of stout.

She looked gravely at them and wagged her finger, swaying slightly. "Yiz are too young to be looking for alcohol. Dhrink is the curse of the working classes." She frowned, "Or do I mean dhrink is the work of the curshing classes? Or is curshing the work of the dhrinking clashes? I think thash what I mean. Ish that what I mean?"

They ran away from her and she shouted after them,"Yiz are in a terrible hurry. Now 'member what I said. Dhrink when yiz are curshin'!"

The next man was full of sympathy, "The Ivy? Oh, I know it well. Looking for your da, are yiz? I s'pose your ma sent yiz to fetch him. Turn right at the end of this road, down the first back alley on your left and there you are. The Ivy. Not the safest place in town mind you. Still, better to fetch your da before he gets into a fight." He paused and became somewhat emotional. "He's lucky to have a wife who cares and chiselers to look out for him, so he is." For a moment the man was overcome and stopped talking. They took the opportunity to thank him and move away, wondering if all adults out at this time of night were astray in the head.

The Ivy did not look at all safe. It was tucked down a lane, as if in hiding. Dim gaslight lit the interior and from time to time shifty individuals slipped in and out, always looking around in case they might be followed.

When the coast was clear Rosie and the twins crept to the doorway. Peering in, it didn't take them long to find Donnelly. He was standing at the bar, shouting, ordering more whiskeys, telling everyone what a good night's work he'd done.

"Best night ever," he shouted. "Best work ever."

The chest was on the bar in front of him.

"What did you do, then?" A weaselly-looking man beside him asked.

"Never you mind. But I got what was rightfully mine!" He patted the box.

The other fellow edged closer. "And what's so great about that then? What's in it?"

He leaned over, about to lift the lid. Donnelly grabbed his wrist and twisted hard. The man yelped. Donnelly let him go. Then he took the gun from his pocket and waved it about, shouting. "See this, do you? Anyone so much as touches what's mine and he's a dead man."

The murmur of conversation died and the weaselly fellow slunk away. Suddenly and for good measure, Donnelly fired a shot at the ceiling. The sound was enormous in the silence. He looked around snarling, then he swallowed his drink, took the chest and left.

"Tom Hannigan said Donnelly isn't as watchful when he's had a few drinks." Rosie sounded dismayed and went on, "But he's watching that gold like a hawk."

"Still," Henry said, "he was a bit foolish to fire that gun, drawing attention to himself – and the chest."

They shrunk into the darkness as Donnelly came out, which was just as well, for while the man was not watching out for them, he was aware of the fortune he carried and the danger of the streets. Every so often he looked around suddenly, hoping to catch out anyone who might be a threat. But the three were cautious, knowing well how dangerous he was and he never saw them.

"Do you think he's drunk?" Rosie whispered. "Maybe we could rush up and barge into him. We could snatch the box."

"What about the gun?" Edward said.

"His aim mightn't be too good." Henry sounded more hopeful than convinced.

They had no doubt that Donnelly would shoot them if he could. He kept to the back alleys and time and time again they were about to rush him when he looked around or their courage failed.

At last the network of lanes finished and he stepped out into a main street. It was here his luck failed. Giving one last, lingering look backwards, Donnelly failed to see the man crossing his path until it was too late and he had stumbled into him and dropped the gun.

"Get out of my way!" he snarled.

"Sorry – hey! Hang on! You're the villain who tried to burn me and those kids!"

It was the night-watchman, on his way home at last, after making his statement to the police. Now his fury gave him extra strength and he gripped Donnelly and shook him. "Help!" he called. "This is the man who burned Arthur Jones!"

Some passers-by came running over.

"Let's get the box!" Henry shouted. They rushed headlong out of the lane into Donnelly. The watchman was already pummelling him, and now, with the added shock of this attack, Donnelly dropped the box.

At once Rosie lifted it and the three of them raced back into the alley.

By now the passers-by were helping the watchman, who hadn't even noticed the three, so quickly had they come and gone.

A policeman turned the corner and blew his whistle long and loud. Excitedly the watchman explained events. "This blackguard tried to murder not just me but some kids too. Only they disappeared. But I saw him before he got away and so did others."

He shook Donnelly hard, "There are witnesses to what you did!" The villain was twisting and turning but could not escape.

"Where's my gold?" he yelled. "Where's the box?"

"What are you on about? There's no gold! Trying to let on you've been robbed, are you? Well, that won't work. No one else is the blackguard here!"

In the alley Rosie and the twins watched as more policemen arrived. Explanations were again given and at last Donnelly was handcuffed and led away.

It was very late by the time they were climbing over the back gate once more. They sneaked up the garden and tried the kitchen door. To their surprise and delight, it opened. In the alcove Rosie set down the chest and they took off their jackets and boots.

"We're very lucky," Edward said. "Cook usually would never forget to lock up."

"And she didn't this time either, you young ruffians!"

Suddenly the light went on and Cook was standing there grimly, arms folded.

They stood there gaping. Then Edward groaned. Did their

parents know? The same thought occured to Henry. "Oh Lord," he sighed. "We're for it now."

"Thought you'd go off scallywagging?" Cook said. "Thought you'd bring your cousin out for a bit of night-time rambling?"

Heads bowed, they didn't answer.

"Next time you'd better oil that gate. You put my heart crossways, so you did. I nearly dropped the supper tray coming back into the kitchen to hear that old gate whining. Thought it was a villain coming in. Only it wasn't, was it? No. It was three villains going out! And here I've been, sitting ever since waiting for you. So what have you been up to?"

It was Rosie who said, "We went into town. To Stephen's Green."

She was surprised to see Cook's face soften.

"Ah. Couldn't wait till tomorrow to see all the lights. The young have no patience." Curiosity got the better of her. "Is it as wonderful as they say?"

They had been so caught up in their adventure they hadn't noticed.

"It's beautiful, Cook," Edward told her. "You should see it. Coloured lights everywhere."

"And the shops? Grafton Street?" Cook was avid.

"Magical," said Henry.

Cook nodded, satisfied for the moment.

"Up to bed with you, now. Be glad I haven't said a word to your parents. Mr O'Neill looked so tired when he came home, I hadn't the heart to inform him. Off with you. Very quietly."

They looked at each other. It wouldn't be wise to pick up the chest. They crept upstairs, Cook following.

Rosie managed to whisper, "I'll go and get the box in a while."

Later she sneaked down. Putting the light on in the kitchen, she went to the alcove. The chest wasn't there.

She gasped. Someone had taken the gold! For a moment she imagined Donnelly had come back. Then, more probably, Cook had found it. But she would've said, wouldn't she? Panic and dismay set in.

Maybe Cook hadn't locked up again before she'd followed them up the stairs. Maybe a robber had sneaked in and taken it.

The three of them had gone through so much to find the treasure and now it had disappeared! Rosie couldn't bear it.

She stood staring at the empty space, willing it to come back. Then she almost jumped out of her skin as behind her Joseph said softly, "Don't worry, Rosie. I've got it. Come into the sitting-room."

She followed him and sat down at the small table where he'd placed the box.

"I have a habit since the twins were babies," he told her, "of checking their rooms last thing before I go to bed. I like to know that all is well. They're always asleep, so they don't know I do it."

She said nothing and he continued, "When they weren't in bed, I checked your room. And when you weren't there I guessed you must have gone after the treasure. I'm right, aren't I? You brought the clues back with you? That's why you came. For the gold."

His expression was sad and she said quickly, "I came because Donnelly was dangerous. I suppose I thought if I gave him the clues he'd leave you alone. Then I showed Edward and Henry and –"

" – And they thought it would be a grand adventure if the three of you solved the puzzle. But Donnelly will be twice as dangerous now, Rosie, if he finds out you've got the gold – *his* gold as he thinks of it!"

"No, he won't." She explained the events of the night, her eyes shining at the memory.

Joseph was not so impressed. Expression sombre, he said slowly, "I'm glad I didn't tell Louisa. This would upset her so much. You could have been burnt to death, Rosie! All three of you could have died. And now you'll have to explain to the police about the sovereigns and tell them you broke into that shop."

"We don't have to tell them. There are loads of witnesses who saw Donnelly at the scene. The police won't need us to put him in prison. No one knows who we are."

Joseph stared at her. "So you plan to keep the money." He looked disappointed.

"No, we don't. Do you know who it belongs to?"

"It belongs to no one. The man Donnelly killed for it had no relatives apparently, and he made no will. So the sovereigns are yours, if you want them."

For a moment Rosie thought about it. The sovereigns would be worth a fortune in 2000. She could be well off for a very long time, buy all the CD's she wanted; go to any rock concert; have whatever clothes she liked; bring Mum and Dad on a holiday to Paris, go to Disney World . . .

Mum and Dad! She came back to earth. How would she explain a fortune in sovereigns to them? She could say she found them, maybe in the back garden, but they'd insist on reporting it to the police or someone. It would get too complicated.

She sighed and Disney World faded.

"They're no good to me," she told Joseph. "Maybe Edward and Henry –"

"The boys have all they need." Joseph was absolute.

Rosie was inspired, "Then give them to Tom Hannigan!"

Joseph's face immediately brightened. "What a wonderful idea," he said. He took it in and beamed at Rosie. "Tom could do with a bit of good luck. The money will help improve his health, give him and his sister a better place to live. Give him some comfort in old age. He could go abroad if he wanted. It's a marvellous plan, Rosie!"

Rosie felt like a genius. His pleasure was infectious and she smiled back at him, "Oh well. I'll get to Disney World some year."

"What?"

"Nothing." She yawned, suddenly jaded.

"Time for a few hours sleep, Rosie. We'll have a great day tomorrow – today, I mean. It's four am on the 4th of April, 1900 and it's a wonderful day in Irish History. It will be a day to remember!"

No it won't, she thought. She did not recall even a sentence about it in her school History book.

When she fell asleep she didn't dream of Victoria, or Donnelly, or gold sovereigns. She dreamed of Disney World.

Chapter 18

Wednesday, 4th April, 1900.

The sun shone in a clear blue sky and that morning, everywhere in Dublin, people were getting ready to welcome the Old Lady. There was an air of celebration, with the city dressed up for the occasion. From very early, extra trains chugged into every station from all over the country. On their journeys, people who had never met before laughed and joked like old friends. Children wore red, white and blue ribbons and hats. They swopped flags and admired photos of the Queen and her family. Adults said what a pity it was that Her Majesty's eldest son, the Prince of Wales, was in Paris and would miss the festivities. Still, the Prince of Connacht was here and some of the princesses.

The whole population was going to the same party and no one was regarded as a stranger.

It was a great day for Ireland. Everybody said so.

Cook and Mollie certainly thought so. They had the day off and were meeting their own friends in the city.

The twins thought so and came down to breakfast waving

small Union Jacks, wearing badges with the letters V R on them. "For Victoria Regina," they told Rosie." *Regina* is Latin for Queen." They offered one to Rosie. She wondered should she wear it out of politeness. For some reason she thought of Mr Yeats and refused.

They didn't mind. "That's all right. She's not your Queen," Henry said.

Joseph suggested the family walk into town. It wasn't too far and that way they'd have time to look at everything. Her Majesty, who was leaving Kingstown at half past eleven, would hardly get to the city before the afternoon and they would be on their stand in College Green long before that.

Although the trams and carriages were full, a lot of people had the same idea as Joseph. There was almost a procession of families making their way into town and they hailed each other along the way.

"Beautiful weather, don't you think!"

"Oh, fit for royalty!"

"Isn't it a great day for Ireland all the same?"

The streets were a sea of red, white and blue as flags and streamers rippled from every window, railing and lamppost. And all along the route there were stands, draped in red, decorated with flowers and pictures of the Queen. At regular intervals bands were setting up. Soldiers in their regimental uniforms were getting into place, lining the kerbside, ready to give the royal salute.

"We'll go down Clyde Road," Joseph said. "It should be especially colourful."

"How could it be any more colourful than this?" Rosie wondered.

"Because all the people who live there got together," Joseph told her, "and they hired a firm of architects to plan and carry out the decorations. It's been written about in all the papers."

No wonder! Rosie thought as they turned down Clyde Road.

Every balcony was draped in scarlet and decorated with the letters V R at least four foot high and picked out in flowers. Where there were no balconies, stands had been erected in the front gardens, all of them draped with Union colours and festooned with greenery and arum lillies. And every house had its flags and bunting in honour of the day. The colours and the flowers matched all along Clyde Road and the result was spectacular.

They walked on towards town by way of Fitzwilliam Place because Joseph had heard about Sir Edmund Bewley's house and wanted to see it. He was not the only one. They joined a small crowd and stared. Over the main entrance was the royal coat of arms and underneath, in fancy scrollwork the words, *Royal Dublin Fusiliers*. Flags and trophies made the whole design sensational.

Every one in Dublin was Queen-mad, Rosie thought. Then in Grafton Street she saw a large placard.

TORCHLIGHT PROCESSION TONIGHT
JOIN PROTEST
AGAINST THE ENGLISH QUEEN

And another one nearby read:

WHOEVER CHEERS FOR QUEEN VICTORIA
DISHONOURS IRELAND

There were more of them, outside shops and attached to lampposts. A horsedrawn van drew up and half a dozen policemen jumped out. Swiftly they dumped the placards into the van. Then one of them spotted a young man and woman handing out leaflets. "Hoy!" he shouted. "You there!" He blew his whistle and the couple started moving rapidly down the street, still trying to hand out leaflets. Those who didn't know what they were took one, but a lot refused.

The young man offered one to Rosie. He was almost running now to avoid the police. She reached out and took it. "Bravo!" he said and quickened his pace.

Again the policeman blew his whistle. Now the six men in uniform were after the young couple. Rosie saw the girl turn down Duke Street. She hid her stack of leaflets in a doorway, then stood calmly fixing her hat, looking casually in a shop window. Two policemen flew by her and as soon as they'd disappeared from sight, the girl picked up her papers and continued with her mission. Rosie hoped the young man was as lucky.

At College Green they took their seats on a huge stand. Outside Trinity a band played all the popular tunes of the day and Rosie was surprised to hear her mother's favourite, "*Abdallah Bulbul Ameer*". The crowd started singing and Rosie was suddenly so homesick she joined in:

And the bravest by far in the ranks of the Tsar was Ivan Skavinsky Skavar
But he caused such great woe when he trod on the toe
Of Abdullah Bul Bul Ameer.

She managed to put everyone out of tune. Louisa groaned and the twins took a fit of laughter. Beside her Joseph closed his eyes. A woman behind Rosie said, "Someone should stop that girl. We came here to be entertained, not tormented. If Her Majesty heard that screeching, she might well take a turn!"

Scarlet, Rosie stopped at once and those around her breathed more easily.

Perhaps deciding it was safer if no one joined in, the band began to play military marches and Rosie switched off, thinking of home.

Joseph bent his head close to hers. "I spoke to the twins

this morning," he said. "They agree the sovereigns should go to Tom Hannigan and I'll see to it tomorrow."

She nodded, and he went on, "They are very impressed with your time-travel, Rosie."

Was he cross that she'd told them?

"It was the only way I could explain how I had the clues," she said.

"I'm glad you told them. Otherwise they wouldn't understand why they might never see you again."

Once more Rosie felt sad, this time for a different reason. "I'll miss them," she said. "And you."

"Yes. We didn't get much time together. But Rosie, you probably saved my life. I didn't realise how dangerous Donnelly was until he tried to murder you and the boys. And if you hadn't come back he would have attempted to kill me when he didn't get the clues. I don't doubt that now."

He stopped, his face strained.

Rosie thought of the years ahead. What would happen to Joseph and his family? She knew nothing of them beyond 1900. There were no family records. Would the boys take part in the huge war that was coming? Her History book said hundreds of thousands had died then. Should she tell Joseph? A warning might protect his sons, especially Edward who was so keen on war. Otherwise they could die and she could not bear the thought of it.

Turning to Joseph, she was about to speak, when he said, "I know life is different in your time, Rosie. And that Ireland is different. But I've served in the British army and it gave me the means to do well. I'll always be loyal to Britain. And so will my sons."

He said it quietly and firmly and she knew if she told him about the Great War, it wouldn't protect him or the twins. He would want to save England, not himself or his family. Better to say nothing. He would only worry.

"I'm going home tomorrow, Joseph," she said instead.

He patted her arm, "I'm very thankful you came back," he sighed. "I always knew you couldn't stay. It's been good to see you again, even if only for such a short time."

And Rosie decided that was their farewell. It would be too painful to say goodbye the next day.

At that moment there was a ripple of excitement. The murmur grew louder and the crowd began to clap and cheer. The royal procession made its way down Grafton Street.

As the horses turned at College Green, earl, countess, duchess, prince and princesses waved at the cheering crowd, escorted by a Guards Regiment on horseback.

In the royal carriage, an old woman raised her hand to greet her subjects. Then she was gone, the horses trotting up Dame Street on the way to the Phoenix Park.

"What a glorious occasion!" said the woman behind Rosie."Truly a great day for Ireland."

Not allowed to move for another three quarters of an hour, the crowd sang with gusto as the bands played "God Save the Queen". It was after five when at last they could go. Policemen shouted, "Walk on your right-hand side only, please! Right-hand side only!"

Rosie had never seen so many people in her life.

They stopped to look in the windows of Switzers and Brown Thomas, where, in spite of the daylight, a blaze of lights lit up window displays dedicated to Her Majesty. Soon they were pushed on by the pressure of people building up behind them.

Street vendors sold their wares, shouting, "Get your badges here! Our nation's heroes here! Lord Kitchener and Lord Roberts only thrupence!"

Joseph brought them to Morrison's Hotel for a grand

evening meal and when it was dark they strolled around the city streets, empty of all traffic so people could see the illuminations. Rosie noticed how happy everyone seemed, laughing as they strolled, now and then stopping to chat with other groups. They ran into neighbours and twice they met the Nelligan boys. Later Mollie hailed them from across the street. She was with some girls her own age, all of them in high spirits.

They met Cook, linking a man in his forties. She blushed beetroot to see them. "Oh sir, Ma'am. Let me introduce you to Daniel Fogarty, a friend."

"Good evening,"said Daniel Fogarty. "Pleased to meet you I'm sure."

"Likewise," said Joseph. "And have you enjoyed the day?"

"How could I do otherwise?" Daniel cried enthusiastically. "Sure twas a wonderful day. A day to remember," he said. "A great day for Ireland!"

And off they went, arm in arm.

On the way home, they had a supper of pork pies from a stall. No one spoke until they'd finished, then Rosie said, "That was the most beautiful pork pie I've ever tasted." She sighed with satisfaction.

She walked with the twins, ahead of their parents who were deep in talk, Joseph's arm resting lightly on his wife's back.

"I'm going home tomorrow," Rosie told the boys. They looked at her in disappointment.

"Do you have to?" Edward asked.

"We were having great fun," Henry said.

"And you're not a bit like Amelia Smith," added his brother.

"What's that got to do with anything?" Rosie said.

"We thought all girls were like Amelia," Henry explained.

"I have to go," Rosie said. "What would I do if I stayed here?"

It wasn't a serious question, but the boys thought it was and eagerly answered.

"You could live with us."

"You could go to school."

"You'd make friends."

"You'd grow up and get married and we'd always know you. You'd be like our sister."

Rosie shook her head. "Louisa would find out I'm not Jane's daughter. She'd never believe the truth. And I like my own school. I don't want to learn embroidery and manners. I want to go to University and maybe do Engineering."

They said, as she had known they would, "But girls can't do that."

"They can in 2000. Anyway, I miss home. I miss Mum and Dad and my friends."

It wasn't an argument they could answer, but they tried. "But if you go, won't you miss us?"

"This isn't my home," she said. "I have to leave. If you want, you can say goodbye."

As it dawned on them what she meant, they cheered up immensely.

"You mean we'll see you disappear? Smashing!" Henry's face lit up.

"Perhaps I'll learn how to do it," Edward was dead keen. "It'd be a great tactic. Especially in Mr Gregson's Latin class."

By the time they got home, the twins were almost looking forward to Rosie's departure.

Chapter 19

NEXT MORNING, very early, Rosie and the twins sneaked out of the house. There was no one on Sandymount Avenue. The servants were sleeping in after the hectic holiday and people were taking their time about going to work.

Rosie put her rucksack on her back and clutched her torch and CD player.

Solemnly the boys insisted on shaking hands.

"Do you think we'll ever meet again?" Henry said.

"Well, I met Joseph again."

They smiled and she did not tell them of her belief that she could only come back when someone belonging to her was in desperate trouble. If life went well for Edward and Henry she would never see them again.

"I've got to go," she said. They nodded.

Just as she closed her eyes, she heard footsteps. It was Joseph.

"Rosie. I want you to take someting with you. So you'll never forget us."

"I wouldn't. Not ever."

"All the same." He handed her a framed photograph of his family. It was the one from the sitting-room.

It was taken against a cloth backdrop. Louisa and Joseph sat side by side, backs straight, the twin standing behind. In the fashion of the day, none of them smiled. Yet they looked happy, a close family.

"I hope you're always like this," Rosie said.

"Don't be daft," Henry told her. "We can't stay the same."

"Well. This is how I'll always see you."

They smiled awkwardly, knowing the time had come, yet wanting to delay it.

She put the photo in her haversack. "I've got to go," she said again.

"Of course you do," Joseph said.

"Say goodbye to Louisa for me." She knew he would think of some excuse for her leaving.

He nodded. She looked at the three of them together and swallowed. "Take care," she told them.

"Bye, Rosie," Henry said.

"We'll see you again sometime," Edward told her.

"Maybe."

Joseph gripped her hand for a moment, then stepped back. "All the best, Rosie," he said, and then repeated softly, "All the best."

This time when she closed her eyes there was no interruption. She held the CD player and the torch and concentrated. She thought of Mum and Dad, of Helena and even of David Byrne. All the time, in the silence of that April morning, her mind chanted the number 2000, over and over again.

She could see her home in Whitehall and imagined stepping through the gate and up the garden path. In her mind she saw the hall, and the quality of the air around her began to change, to hum with far-off sounds. She pictured all the rooms in the house. She heard a rushing sound, like the noise of traffic, yet still far off. The rooms faded and the noise was suddenly much louder, much closer.

She blinked.

Joseph and the boys were gone and she was standing on Sandymount Avenue in the middle of the morning rush-hour, dressed as she had been a week before.

"Did you have a good time, Rosie?" Mum asked, almost as soon as she walked in the door.

"It was great," she said, and added mischievously, "You wouldn't believe it."

"By the way, before I forget, David Byrne called about an hour ago."

Rosie's heart sank. "What did he want?"

"Oh, apparently he was on holidays himself. He brought you back a present." She produced a brown paper parcel, very lumpy.

Heart in her mouth, Rosie opened it to find a snorkel and flippers and a note.

Mum was looking puzzled, "What does he say?"

"He says, 'These are for the sea, next time you go to Wexford in April. David.'"

"What a strange boy. Who'd want to go swimming in the sea in April?"

Upstairs she unpacked her rucksack and studied the photo. It had faded a good deal. The twins looked at her across the century, their faces serious, but at the same time eager and hopeful. Rosie could not imagine anything bad happening to them. They would always see life as a marvellous adventure. They would be fine. They would always look out for each other. A weight lifted.

She had done what she set out to do and it was time to stop worrying about them.

Glancing at the snorkel and flippers on the bed, she smiled.

Suddenly she was looking forward to going back to school and hearing how David Byrne got on in Wexford.

The End